Mitch looked all the way down to her toes and back up again to her eyes.

Normally Kinsey didn't give a flip what other people thought of her looks, but she wanted to meet with Mitch's approval. Silence stretched out between them as he devoured her.

He moved so fast she hardly had time to jump. But all of a sudden he loomed before her, blacker than the night and more dangerous than sin. His hands were on her, climbing up her back, drawing her against him.

His gaze dropped to her mouth, then lifted back to her eyes. He murmured, his voice a low, tight rumble.

"I'm going to spend the entire evening imagining ripping that dress off you, throwing you down and making love to you until you scream."

Dear Reader,

Welcome to the H.O.T. WATCH! I'm so excited to get to share this new series with you! Over my years of working with and writing about Special Forces operatives, I've always been fascinated by their real-life, yet nearly superhuman qualities. And now you and I get to really explore that aspect of these amazing warriors.

As I sat down to plan this series, I asked myself, how am I going to do justice to this elite group of operatives? First I decided to give them a cool hideout full of high-tech gadgets. Then I had to give them some seriously evil bad guys to battle. After all, a hero is only as awe-inspiring as the villain he defeats.

Of course, I had to throw in plenty of steamy tropical islands, sultry nights, pounding surf and glistening muscles. Add a heaping helping of sex appeal, and we have a recipe for plenty of yummy fun. So get out your beach towel and suntan lotion and pour yourself a tall, cool drink. Then prepare to be swept away by the supermen and women of H.O.T. WATCH!

All my best,

Cindy

THE DARK SIDE
OF NIGHT

Cindy Dees

Silhouette®

Romantic
SUSPENSE

SILHOUETTE BOOKS

ISBN-13: 978-0-373-27579-3
ISBN-10:   0-373-27579-X

THE DARK SIDE OF NIGHT

Books by Cindy Dees

Silhouette Romantic Suspense

CINDY DEES

started flying airplanes while sitting in her dad's lap at the age of three and got a pilot's license before she got a driver's license. At age fifteen, she dropped out of high school and left the horse farm in Michigan where she grew up to attend the University of Michigan.

After earning a degree in Russian and East European studies, she joined the U.S. Air Force and became the youngest female pilot in the history of the Air Force. She flew supersonic jets, VIP airlift and the "C-5" Galaxy, the world's largest airplane. She also worked part-time gathering intelligence. During her military career, she traveled to forty countries on five continents, was detained by the KGB and East German secret police, got shot at, flew in the first Gulf War, met her husband and amassed a lifetime's worth of war stories.

Her hobbies include professional Middle Eastern dancing, Japanese gardening and medieval reenacting. She started writing on a one-dollar bet with her mother and was thrilled to win that bet with the publication of her first book in 2001. She loves to hear from readers and can be contacted at www.cindydees.com.

This book is for my real-life superhero friends
whose names I cannot print. You know who you are.
And may I just say, you ROCK!

For my mom and mother-in-law,
who in their courageous battles with cancer
have taught me that life's short, live hard.

Chapter 1

Smoking gun in hand, Mitch Perovski crouched over the crumpled form of the dead man and swore. One by one, droplets of blood plopped onto the boat's deck in the charged silence. Glancing furtively around him for watching eyes, he crouched even lower and pulled out his cell phone.

"Go ahead," a male voice said at the other end.

"Lancer here," he muttered. "I've got a problem. My Plan B is dead, I'm caught out in the open at a damned marina, and I've got two, possibly three, gunmen on my tail. I need you guys to pull a rabbit out of your hats and get me the hell out of here."

"We've got you on the satellite map in a marina near the south end of Tortola. The boss man says to stay put for a minute if you can. Meanwhile, say your status."

For a moment, Mitch allowed himself to register the

daggers of pain shooting from his left shoulder. Bad idea. He gritted his teeth, forced the agony back into a mental drawer, and slammed it shut. No time for that, yet. "I'm shot," he ground out. "My left shoulder. I think the bullet passed through but I haven't had time to stop and take a look. I'm low on ammo and way exposed on this freaking dock."

"Are you bleeding?" the combat controller asked sharply.

"Hell, yes, I'm bleeding. I just took a bullet."

"Apply pressure to the entrance and exit wounds with a clean pad, and hold it until the bleeding stops."

"Gee, thanks, Doctor Kildaire. I had no idea what to do," Mitch retorted dryly. All the guys in the H.O.T. Watch were qualified EMTs.

"Standard procedure to brief operatives on proper first aid when a wound is reported," the controller replied, equally as dry. "That way when you die, your family can't sue us over your sorry ass."

Mitch snorted. He hadn't spoken to any member of the Perovski clan in close to ten years and didn't plan on doing so for at least another ten. The seconds ticked by at half speed while he scanned the area for signs of his pursuers. They weren't showing themselves at the moment, but he didn't doubt for an instant that they were out there, waiting. Seconds turned into minutes, and he wondered how much longer his pursuers would sit tight. Eventually, they would run out of patience and come after him. He was dead meat if they caught him out here like this.

A new, deeper voice finally came on the line. "Lancer, this is White Horse." *His temporary boss.*

Navy Commander Brady Hathaway. "I've got a Plan C for you. About a half mile down the beach, Congressman Dick Hollingsworth has a vacation home. He has a fast boat, and I just got off the horn with him. He's given you permission to use it. The spare ignition key is taped to the back of a painting of a clipper ship in the below-deck cabin. You'll have to break into the cabin, though. I told him we'll repair any damage you do to the door."

A half mile? Damn, that sounded like a long way right now. "What does the boat look like?" Mitch bit out.

"It's a thirty-eight foot cigarette. And——" was that a wince he heard in Lancer's voice? His boss continued "—it's pink. Named *Baby Doll.* But it goes like a bat outta hell, apparently."

"It had better," Mitch growled. "If I die in a pink boat, I'm going to haunt you. And I won't be a nice ghost."

White Horse laughed shortly. "Call us when you're safe. And take care of that shoulder when you get a chance."

"Will do." Mitch tucked the cell phone in his pocket and briefly considered swimming for the pink boat. But his shoulder was throbbing like hell, and the idea of adding the burn of salt in the wound was more than even his pain tolerance would stand. He eased down the dock, staying low. If his luck held, he could sneak into that fringe of palmettos and bushes up the beach, and then make his way to the pink Plan C.

If his luck held.

Just another lousy day in paradise. Kinsey sighed and sat up. She'd spent the entire afternoon napping on the cigarette boat's sleek hull, which rocked gently beneath her as the waves rolled in. A strip of white sand beach stretched away in both directions, fringed by rustling palm trees and kissed by turquoise seas so blue they almost hurt to look at.

As dull as it was down here, it was still better than being laughed at. Laughed at! Her. The darling of Newport society. She'd fled rather than face the cruel scorn of the country club crowd and those who called themselves her friends. In a few months, when the scandal had been eclipsed by some new sensation, maybe she'd think about going home. But until then, she was hunkering down here at her father's beach house. Okay, she'd admit it, she was hiding.

The sun was beginning to dip toward the horizon. Not quite sunset, but the day's quality tanning time was over. She didn't feel like going inside yet, though. Maybe a spin in the *Baby Doll* would clear her head. She pulled a T-shirt on over her skimpy bikini and, jumping over to the pier, cast off the forward mooring line. She strolled down the dock to cast off the aft line.

A rapid, slapping sound made Kinsey look over her shoulder sharply. Feet striking the dock. Urgent. Staccato. *Running full out.* Nobody ran around here. It was too hot and humid in this tropical climate—too damned languid—for anything so strenuous.

A tall man was charging down the long pier straight at her. Dark hair. Broad shoulders. Black clothes from head to foot. Bulky black duffel bag slung over his right shoulder. As mesmerizing—and lethal—as a panther charging on the attack. He never even slowed as he twisted to look behind him. She glanced in the direction of his gaze. Two more men were coming on the run...brandishing *guns*.

She leaped into the boat's open cockpit, searching frantically for the keys. Where in heck had she put them? There they were. In a cup holder. She dived for them, prayed she'd grabbed the right key, and jabbed it at the ignition. *Missed!* She tried again.

Four thuds in quick succession made her duck instinctively. What was that noise? Whatever it was, it sounded bad.

The *Baby Doll*'s three Merc 700 horsepower motors turned over with a single smooth rumble. The man with the duffel bag was almost on her. She threw the engines into gear and yanked hard on the steering wheel. The boat pivoted around practically in place, the rear hull digging deep into the water.

As the *Baby Doll* exploded away from the dock, a dark shape went airborne, crashing onto the boat's deck behind her. Kinsey jerked violently. *The guy in black.* She started to throttle back.

"Go!" he shouted from where he sprawled. She hesitated, and he shouted, "Hit it, lady! You and I are both dead if they catch us!"

Wha—? She slammed the throttles forward while her brain hitched and stumbled, tripping over itself. *Dead? Both* of them? What had *she* done to merit getting killed? The boat shot forward like a thoroughbred bursting out of the chute, slamming her back into the pilot's form-fitting leather seat. In the time it took Kinsey to jerk in a startled breath and release it, the *Baby Doll* had accelerated to nearly seventy miles per hour.

Kinsey risked a glance at the man crawling into the seat beside her. His hair was black-coffee brown, his skin bronze—by sun or genetics, she couldn't tell. He looked Italian in an elegant, lounge-around-a-Tuscan villa way. He righted himself and commenced fishing in his duffel bag. His left sleeve was ripped at the shoulder seam and—holy cow—blood gleaned wetly over the tear.

"Who are you?" she shouted over the roar of the engines. She sincerely hoped this man was the good guy in that little chase scene back at the dock; otherwise, she could be in a world of hurt, alone and on the open ocean with a potentially violent man. Heck, even if he *was* the good guy, she could very well be in deep trouble.

He looked over at her. Their gazes locked and time stopped for an instant, the power of that split second staggering. His eyes were amber. As gold as the sunset beginning to form in the west and positively hypnotic. *Was he the cop or the robber?* No telling by his dangerous good looks. A distant roar behind them sounded like an angry lion.

"Here they come." His voice was raspy from exertion and sent an involuntary shiver down her spine.

She glanced back toward shore. A boat was just pulling away from the next dock over, another long, sleek cigarette.

"Who are they?" she shouted.

He stared grimly over her shoulder at the cigarette roaring toward them. His reply was succinct. "Hired killers."

Terror rushed over her; cold certainty that death was very near. Her legs abruptly felt unbearably restless and she restrained an impulse to jump up and run away.

"Can we outrun them?" he asked.

She took a closer look at the boat pursuing them. A forty-three or forty-four foot SuperVee. "Nope. This boat tops out around eighty-five miles per hour. That one will push a hundred."

His metallic gaze swung back to her. It was cold. Utterly devoid of emotion. And that scared her worst of all. There wasn't any question of not doing exactly what he told her.

"Then we'll stand and fight."

The link between reality and the nightmare unfolding around her stretched. Broke. *Fight?* The synapses between her conscious thoughts and having any idea what to do next shut down. Completely.

"How good a driver are you?" he demanded, yanking her back from the void.

She answered without even thinking. She'd been around water and boats since she was born. "Very good."

"Can you get me close enough to that boat to shoot at it?"

"Get close? Intentionally?" she squeaked.

"Yes. So I can shoot them," he repeated impatiently.

Shoot? As in guns and bullets? *Was she about to die?* The thought gave a terrible clarity to every breath, every sound. Her hands gripped the contoured steering wheel until they ached.

"Damn," her passenger muttered. "He's got an angle on us."

If she could've forced words past the panic paralyzing her throat, she might have asked who "he" was and why having an angle sounded bad. But then her passenger reached into the duffel at his feet and pulled out a short, thick machine gun. *Oh. My. God.*

"Turn right!" he ordered tersely.

Kinsey yanked the wheel, and the nimble boat whipped around so hard it made her neck hurt. The *Baby Doll* slashed across the path of the black cigarette at nearly a right angle.

A flash of light exploded beside her. A burst of rattling, deafening sound. Her passenger had fired his gun at the other boat! As the other vessel passed behind them, he whirled and fired again.

"Bring us around for another pass!" he shouted. "Keep our nose or tail pointed at him and don't give him our broadside if you can help it."

Abjectly grateful for something to think about besides dying, her panicked brain kicked into overdrive. The sailor in her latched on to the problem his instructions posed. His orders were easier said than done. And frankly, she'd rather have the bastards shooting toward her pointed prow and the compact living quarters inside it than at her stern where the engines…and gas tanks…were housed.

The black boat slowed abruptly and turned hard to face them. Its engines roared a challenge. Coming in for a head-on pass, like a knight on a black charger. She dared not get into a contest of straight runs against the larger, faster boat. It would eat them alive. She had to keep them both going in circles. Use her more agile boat and tighter turn radius to her advantage. Keep speed out of the mix altogether.

The other boat accelerated. Coming straight at them. Her passenger grabbed the top of the short windshield to steady himself and his weapon.

"Don't get comfortable," she called. "I'm going to turn hard right just in front of him and you'll get a better shot to your left. We're going to send up a hell of a wake and it's going to rock him violently, so time your shots accordingly."

He spared her a startled glance. Then he grinned at her, a fleeting expression that passed across his face almost too fast to see. But she caught the flash of white, the sexy lift of the corner of his mouth. His eyes briefly glowed whiskey-warm—and then the smile was gone. He was gone. With a bunch and spring of powerful thighs, he'd leaped aft to crouch behind the seats.

The distance between the two boats closed shockingly fast. She made out the face of the other boat's driver, a swarthy man with death in his eyes. A second man stood up in the passenger's seat, brandishing some sort of machine gun over the windshield.

He wasn't looking at her, though. He was searching the deck of her vessel for her passenger. The black boat's engines roared even louder. Obviously the other driver expected to make a straight, high-speed pass and let the gunmen duke it out.

Wrongo, buckwheat. Just a few more seconds… almost…*there!* She yanked off the throttles and whipped the steering wheel over to the right, standing the *Baby Doll* up practically on her starboard side. As the port propeller came back down in the water, Kinsey jammed in the power. The boat leaped forward, up and over its own wake. Her prow slammed down and stabilized, giving her passenger a great look at the black boat.

Clearly stunned by her maneuver, the other driver

slammed his throttles back and jerked right to avoid a collision. They'd have never hit…the *Baby Doll* had cut across his path too fast. But the guy's sharp turn combined with her wake hitting him full broadside rocked the big cigarette violently.

The other gunman staggered, grabbing for his windshield and hanging on desperately to avoid getting dumped out of the boat altogether.

"Now!" she screamed.

Her companion popped up, firing hard and fast. The crackling sound of bullets ripping into fiberglass peppered the air. The other gunman lurched left to face them…just in time to clutch at his chest and topple over into the water. Swear to God, it looked like a stunt straight out of a Hollywood movie. Except that rapidly spreading scarlet in the water was no movie prop.

And then the *Baby Doll* danced away, arcing away behind the black cigarette. The other driver craned his neck around, trying to keep her in visual range. His engines roared and the chase was on again. The guy tried to cut off the angle of her curve and come straight at her again, but she hadn't grown up on the water for nothing. She continued turning back and forth until the black cigarette was forced into following the same turning track behind her.

"Hang on," she warned her passenger. "We're about to zig right and hope he zags left!" She whipped her boat into a counterturn, arcing back into the path of the other boat. It was a maneuver an old Vietnam fighter pilot had shown her once. He called it a counterturn. Whatever it was called, it was highly effective. In a matter of seconds, her prow was pointed straight at the black boat's starboard side. Her client jumped up in the passenger seat and raked the black boat with automatic gunfire. Fist-size holes abruptly marred the sleek black hull.

"Lower!" she called. "Down by the water line!"

He didn't acknowledge her instruction. But, he must've changed his aim, for immediately a new line of fissures erupted along the black hull mere inches above the water. The fiberglass cracked and shattered under the relentless spray of lead. She peeled hard left, sending up a rooster tail of water that had to have drenched the other driver. If she was lucky, the other guy's hull should be badly compromised and starting to take on water.

"Get down!" her companion shouted.

She ducked as popping noises burst all around her. The *Baby Doll* shuddered as something—a whole bunch of somethings—hit her. *Not good.* The other gunman was firing back. Kinsey slammed the throttles forward. The *Baby Doll* bounded away from the spray of lead. The sound of the other boat diminished. She looked over her shoulder. The black boat wasn't giving chase. For that matter, it looked to be riding noticeably low in the water.

She guided the *Baby Doll* around a rocky point and the crippled black boat disappeared from view. They raced onward for another two minutes or so, flying down the coast of Tortola, the largest of the British Virgin Islands.

"I've got to slow down and check out my boat soon," she called. Although the *Baby Doll* didn't handle like it was taking on water, it was a half-million-dollar piece of equipment, and it wasn't hers. Her father would kill her if she sank his favorite toy.

"Do it," her passenger replied.

She powered back to idle, and the sudden quiet was a shock. "Take the wheel while I have a look at the hull."

She stepped out of the cockpit and, balancing carefully, made her way out onto the forward hull. She stretched out on her stomach and leaned over the edge of the boat to have a look at the damage. A series of dents marred the cotton-candy-pink hull, but shockingly, it didn't look like there were any holes. Stunned, she shifted over the other side of the boat. No hull breaches there, either. *Thank God.*

"How's it looking?" the man asked.

"Fine," she replied in disbelief. She pressed to her feet and made her way back to the deck.

He offered her a hand as she stepped over the windshield. Their palms met, his large and callused and impossibly gentle. An actual tremor passed through her. And she wasn't a trembly kind of girl, thank you very much. *Wow.* She hopped down, still holding his hand. He waited a millisecond too long to release her fingers. But she noticed. And her stomach did a neat flip.

She cleared her throat nervously. "None of the bullets seem to have punctured the hull. Now that I think about it, I remember hearing something about this boat having a hybrid epoxy hull that uses layers of Kevlar instead of fiberglass or carbon cloth."

Her passenger's eyebrows shot straight up. "A bulletproof boat?"

"Sort of." Belatedly, caution speared through her. "Who are you? And who were those guys chasing you?"

"It doesn't matter. For what it's worth, my employer

will pay for any damage to the boat incurred while you saved my a—" he amended, "my behind."

"Not to worry. Anyone who can afford a boat like this can afford repairs on it." She might have delivered that line in a supremely unconcerned manner, but she was shaking from head to foot. She'd actually been shot at! For that matter, this guy was still casually brandishing his machine gun. He'd slung it from a strap over his right shoulder, and it pointed down the length of his muscular thigh. She jerked her gaze away from his weapon nervously.

She ticked off on her fingers, "Boat chase, check. Gun battle, check. Narrow escape, check. What's next on the agenda, Mister—?" She broke off, leaving the obvious question of his name hanging.

He hesitated just an instant too long. "Perovski. Mitch Perovski."

"For today, at any rate?" she replied lightly.

"Something like that," he responded, as dry as the Gobi desert.

Not much of a talker. But then, she could relate. She'd come down here to the islands in search of silence, herself. Relief from the vapid noise of humanity. "My name's Kinsey—" she hesitated. Rather than give him her well known last name, she substituted her middle name. "—Pierpont. Kinsey Pierpont."

She powered the boat up to a safe and inconspicuous cruising speed, closer to twenty knots than eighty. "Where can I take you?"

He snorted. "Anywhere that's not Tortola, or the British Virgin Islands for that matter."

The *Baby Doll* carried fuel for a few hours of

cruising, which would reach several nearby islands outside the British chain—not that she'd decided to take him anywhere. "Did you kill that guy?" The words were out of her mouth before she could stop them.

He shrugged. "A gut shot like that is usually fatal, but since we didn't stick around to check him out, I wouldn't call it a confirmed kill."

He sounded so bloody calm about it. Her heart practically pounded its way out of her chest at the mere thought of that guy toppling overboard.

"What islands can we reach on our current fuel load?" the man asked, abruptly serious again. He'd gone from relaxed to full predator mode in the blink of an eye. The shift was disconcerting.

She glanced down at the fuel gauges. "Where did you have in mind?"

Another shrug. *Cagey, he was.* "You were the Plan C I wasn't supposed to need. I didn't work out the details after the part where you saved my hide. Thanks, by the way."

"You're welcome, I think. You are one of the good guys, aren't you?"

"I am."

That was it? No explanation? No identification? No reason offered for carrying around that monstrous gun and using it on someone? "And the guy you shot?"

"Definite bad guy."

It would be far too easy to take this man at his word. She needed to believe him. Needed to believe he wouldn't turn that gun on her with the same casual ease he had those other guys. Heck, she *needed* to get on the radio and call the British Coast Guard. She reached for the radio mike and jumped violently when her passenger's hand whipped out to cover hers. His grip wasn't painful, but was unmistakably powerful.

"What are you doing?" His voice was a low, dangerous rumble.

The sound vibrated deep in her belly, stirring part fear and part something else altogether. She replied lightly, "I'm calling in the cavalry."

"Don't."

"But—"

"You don't know what you're involved in. Don't call the authorities or the blood of a whole lot of good men could end up on your hands."

"But those guys were *shooting* at us—"

"And we shot back."

"*You* shot back."

"I shot back. I need you to leave the police out of this for now. I can't go into the details but you have to trust me."

Riiight. Trust him. Not.

"I need you to promise you won't contact the police. I don't want to have to restrain you."

"Restrain—"

He cut her off with a sharp slash of his hand through the air. "Promise."

Their gazes clashed, hers defiant and his...the sun turned his a molten gold that could consume her whole and melt her down to nothing. A girl could lose herself in those eyes if she wasn't careful. Very careful.

"Well?" he demanded. "Do we do this the easy way or the hard way?"

Chapter 2

Her gaze narrowed. Oh, how tempting it was to tell him to go to hell. But he was bigger than she was, stronger than she was, and undoubtedly meaner. Then there was his machine gun to consider. Reining in her surliness, she retorted, "I won't call the police if you'll put that gun away."

He stared intently at her for a moment more, clearly weighing her honesty. Then he nodded. "Fair enough." He pivoted with that extreme, muscular grace of his and padded to the back of the deck where his duffel still lay. She caught the wince that passed across his features.

"Are you okay?" she asked in quick concern. If those guys in the black boat came back, Mitch was her only protection.

"Yeah. It's a flesh wound. I'll clean it up when I know we're safe."

"It looks bad."

He glanced down, surprised. "Nah, that's a little scratch. No organs hanging out or bones showing. I'm good."

He wasn't good—he was hurt.

She watched cautiously as he wiped down the machine gun and stowed it in the canvas bag.

Thank God. Being in the presence of that giant weapon made her too nervous to function rationally. Not to mention, he was gorgeous enough to send her pulse into the stratosphere. Her thoughts jumped around as disjointedly as caged monkeys.

"I know your name, but who are you?" she asked more sharply than she'd intended. Panic hovered too close, waiting for the slightest opening in which to pounce.

"I'm American."

"I can tell you're American from your accent. But who *are* you?"

Silence. A frown wrinkled his brow, but he ignored her question. *Or maybe chose not to answer.*

How rude was that? He'd dragged her into the middle of a shoot-out, for goodness' sake. A tiny voice in the back of her head said her anger was irrational, but the much louder voice of her fear-morphed-to-fury overruled it. "Who were those men chasing you?"

That got more reaction out of him. A full-blown shrug. *Wow. Some communicator.* A flinch flickered across his face, then his expression went smooth and impassive again. Except for those incredible eyes of his. They all but ate her alive.

Her insides quailing with some reaction she chose

not to examine closely, she tried again. "Why were they shooting at you?"

His gaze, now tinted orange by the blossoming sunset, snapped with irritation. What did he have to be irritated about? She was the injured party here. She announced, "I want you off the boat. Now."

"I'll bet you do," he purred.

He could stop sending shivers across her skin like that any time now. "I'm serious."

He glanced around at the water on all sides with distaste. "You want me to jump overboard?"

"I was thinking more in terms of walking the plank. But I want you off the *Baby Doll*. I want no part of whatever it is you're mixed up in."

Dammit, the guy had a smile so hot it threatened to melt her righteous fury into a completely ineffectual puddle of lust. *Spine, woman. Spine!* Her gaze narrowed belatedly.

The humor drained from his expression, abruptly leaving it as cold as the arctic. Dread clawed her gut. Absolutely nothing radiated off him now. Not anger, not irritation, not even danger. He went absolutely, totally, completely still.

"There are sharks in these waters," he finally muttered.

Yeah, and she was looking at the most deadly one of all. Taking a deep breath and mustering up all her courage to stare him down, she replied, "There's no history in this area of shark attacks on humans. I don't want any trouble. Please go. The water's warm and it's only about a quarter mile to shore."

The southwestern tip of Tortola was sliding past their port side now.

He sighed and replied almost soothingly, "I'm sorry. I can't leave you."

"Can't you swim?" she challenged a bit tartly.

Aggravation flashed in his gaze, and matching satisfaction surged in her. He snapped, "I swim very well, thank you. Why, I've swum with—" He broke off. "Look. We have a little problem. The driver of that boat got a good look at you. Too good a look."

"And this is a problem why?"

"Because now he has to kill you."

She huffed in disbelieving laughter. "I've never seen that man in my life! Why in the world would he hurt me?"

Perovski's voice dropped into a careful, reasonable timbre. "I didn't say hurt. I said kill. And he'd do it because he thinks you got too good a look at him."

"I barely caught a glimpse of him what with all the bullets flying and wild driving I was doing."

In an even gentler tone, he replied, "But *he* doesn't know that. For all he knows, you could pick him out of a mug book or a lineup. He can't afford to let you live."

Her jaw dropped. A killer thought she could finger him? She felt a distinct urge to throw up. "Great. Why did I have to get dragged into this?"

Sounding downright apologetic now, he answered, "No one said anything about there being anyone aboard the *Baby Doll*. Congressman Hollingsworth said I could borrow his boat, but he didn't say anything about you being here."

"He doesn't know I'm here."

Perovski started. "Did you *steal* this boat?"

"Of course not! I just didn't tell my father I was coming down to the beach house."

"Your father?" His voice was deadly quiet.

She exhaled hard. "Yeah. My father. Richard Hollingsworth."

He pounced immediately. "I thought you said your name was Kinsey Pierpont."

"It is. Kinsey Pierpont Hollingsworth."

He absorbed that one in silence. So much for anonymity on this little retreat of hers. This guy would brag to someone in a bar about running into Kinsey Hollingsworth, and someone would overhear him. Before she knew it, the local paparazzi would mob her. And any chance at hiding in peace would be blown.

"Your middle name is really Pierpont?"

He didn't have to sound so bloody amused about it. "What's yours?" she challenged.

"Edgar," he admitted.

She suppressed a spurt of laughter. "And you're giving me grief about Pierpont?"

"I'm named after my grandfather," he said defensively.

"So am I," she retorted.

Laughter danced in his eyes, transforming their dangerous depths to a warm, inviting amber. Belatedly, she shook herself free of their spell.

She sighed. "Since you're the reason I've apparently run afoul of the guy in the boat, what do you suggest I do about it?"

He clammed up on her again. It figured. Honestly, the whole idea of some killer tracking her down and offing her was too preposterous. She faced her impromptu companion squarely and said resolutely, "Please leave."

His shoulders bunched up in annoyance, followed by

a grimace of pain, but his voice was a low, steady rumble that made her want to curl up in it. "Ma'am, I'm not kidding. That bastard's gonna kill you."

"He doesn't even know who I am."

"And two minutes on the Internet running the name of this boat or a couple quick phone calls wouldn't produce your identity and enough information to find you and kill you? With all due respect, you're not exactly a low-profile kind of girl."

"Low-profile?" she repeated ominously.

He shrugged. "Yeah. Your dad's famous, and besides, you look...rich. With that lightbulb-blond hair and those legs—" he broke off.

She got the idea. Why the sour note in his voice when he described her, though? She studied him, and he glared back inscrutably. Something primitive deep inside her rose to the challenge of this man, relishing sparring with him.

What the heck was she supposed to do now? Pretend the shooting had never happened and take the *Baby Doll* back to Daddy's place? Run and hide? The pure insanity of such ruminations yanked her rudely back to reality. He was just trying to scare her. Perovski didn't want her to toss him off the boat and was probably making up the whole business of the other shooter coming after her.

He subsided into brooding silence, staring sphinxlike at the sunset's splendor. The moods of the sky were many, and at the moment the evening was quiet. Soft. Contemplative. Streaks of peach and lavender reached toward the east, where the distant horizon was darkening into a blue nearly as deep and unfathomable as the sea around them. Night would come soon. She got the distinct feeling the man beside her was a creature of the dark. An errant desire to walk in that world flashed through her. It might be a more interesting place than the gilded media microscope she lived under.

At least he hadn't threatened her. And his gun was put away. As armed and dangerous night stalkers went, he could've been worse.

St. John, one of the U.S. Virgin Islands, wasn't far away. She could duck into Cruz Bay—the U.S. Coast Guard guys there were on the ball. If she signaled them for help, they'd nab this man and his gun and get them off her boat. And after all, she'd only promised not to call the police. She hadn't said anything about not contacting the Coast Guard. She set course for St. John. Now all she had to do was keep this guy calm until she got there.

She glanced over at him. He slouched in the passenger seat, far too sexy for his own good. She almost missed having not been born in the good old days before AIDS and other nasty STDs, when a girl could casually jump a guy's bones without any thought to consequences. This guy just begged to be bedded.

He leaned his head back against the leather headrest. His eyes drifted closed. For an instant, he looked utterly exhausted. She shifted weight the slightest bit, and his eyes snapped open, alert and intelligent. His gaze traveled briefly up and down the length of her. "Are you done panicking yet?"

She blinked. Retorted with light sarcasm, "Why, yes, I'm perfectly fine. Thank you for asking. Lovely weather we're having, aren't we?"

A rusty sound escaped him. It took her a moment to

identify it. That was a laugh—from a man who apparently didn't do it very often.

"Jeez, that was close," he mumbled.

Keep him talking. Make a human connection with him. So he wouldn't view her as an object to be kidnapped or killed at will. "And just what was *that?*"

"A hit. Or rather an attempted hit, since I'm still alive."

"Why were they trying to kill you?"

He shrugged. "The list of people who'd like to see me dead is long and distinguished."

"Were those old enemies or new ones?"

He shot her a speculative look. "A perceptive question. And one to which I don't know the answer."

Why would someone hire assassins to take this man out? What line of work *was* he in? "You're not a drug dealer, are you? Because I don't mess with drugs, regardless of what the tabloids say. And I certainly won't run them on this boat."

He made a wry face at her. "Trust me. My life would be a helluva lot simpler if I were a drug runner."

"So how do you know my father?"

"I don't."

"And he let you borrow his boat because…"

"Because my boss asked him for a favor. And no, I'm not going to tell you who my boss is."

"Did my father know you were running from hit men when he agreed to this favor?"

Mitch's lips twitched. "He probably surmised as much."

"Why?" She didn't waste her breath asking again what he did, but the question hung heavy in the air between them. Silence stretched out while she waited for an explanation, but none was forthcoming. She probed a little more. "Surely you're exaggerating the threat to me. I vaguely saw two men from a distance and one of them has a giant hole in his chest now. I certainly wasn't close enough to make out their faces."

"You saw more than you know."

"Like what?"

"You can accurately estimate their height and weight. Identify hair color. Skin color. Give a rough description of their clothing. Of how they ran. Their shooting stances. Tell that they used handguns and a shotgun. And if you know anything about firearms, you might be able to tell the police they used large caliber, hollow-point slugs from the sounds of the shots."

She was tempted to swear under her breath. *He was right.* Darn it. She'd just wanted some peace and quiet. To be left alone. Was that too much to ask for? She fiddled with the GPS navigation system, checked the coordinates for St. John, and made a course correction to point more directly at the island and its Coast Guard contingent. They'd remove this guy from her boat and her life, and then, if she was lucky, paradise would settle back down to its dull, safe and monotonous routine.

If she was lucky.

Mitch's cell phone vibrated insistently against his hip. *Again.* Yeah, he bet they wanted to talk to him. In a *big* way. They'd probably picked up a report of a dead man in the water from Coast Guard radio scanners in Tortola. Thank God Kinsey had already been on the *Baby Doll* and had the boat untied and engines running.

Otherwise, he'd be shark bait now instead of the Cuban killer.

Interesting female, Kinsey Hollingsworth. Very East Coast upper crust. The whole package screamed old money. Her attractiveness went way beyond good grooming and expensive packaging. She was genuinely beautiful. Her blue eyes, long blond hair and aristocratic bones were very easy on the eye. She ran to the tall side, maybe five foot eight. In good shape. Just enough curves in the right places to give a man hot sweats. Which set his teeth thoroughly on edge. He probably shouldn't despise every leggy, gorgeous blonde he met, but damned if he could stop the reaction. Even after all these years, the gall of betrayal tasted bitter in his mouth.

At least the princess hadn't panicked when the chips were down.

Nobody should've known about tonight's meeting between him and Zaragosa. How in the hell had the Cubans found out about it? Worse, how had they found out about the meeting early enough to position assassins to disrupt it?

He didn't like it. Not one bit. This was the sort of wrinkle that got a mission scrubbed. But he wasn't so sure the boys upstairs would call this one off. Too much rode on it. And like it or not, he was the best man for the job. Hell, the only man for the job.

He pushed wearily to his feet. He probably ought to see to his shoulder now.

"I need somewhere dry to stow my bag," he announced.

Kinsey replied, "Inside the cabin. There's storage under the sofa cushions."

She turned away to have a look at the propellers, and he took the opportunity to surreptitiously unplug the microphone from the boat's radio. He pocketed it quickly, grabbed his bag, and headed inside.

Sure enough, the bullet had grazed the meaty part of his upper arm just below the shoulder joint. After awkwardly cleaning and bandaging the shallow wound, he fished out his cell phone. He needed to let the boys in the Bat Cave know he was alive and find out if the mission was still green-lighted after this fiasco.

The *Baby Doll*'s cabin was low and compact. A flat-screen TV, tufted leather upholstery, and lots of brushed chrome oozed money. Nearly as sexy and expensive as the woman up top. A tiny porthole let in a wash of red light as he dialed. The phone barely finished a single ring before it was picked up.

"White Horse, here. Go."

Usually, Mitch worked on the civilian side of the house for Jennifer Blackfoot, the civilian agent-in-charge of the Hunter Operation Team. Casually dubbed the H.O.T. Watch. But for this mission, he'd been put under the control of her equivalent on the military side of the operation, Commander Hathaway.

Mitch replied, "Lancer here. Thought you'd like an update."

"It's good to hear your voice."

Mitch snorted. "It's good to be alive. This afternoon was a little too close for me."

"Where are you now?"

"Sitting on the *Baby Doll* in the middle of the Caribbean watching the prettiest sunset you ever saw. Thanks for arranging the Plan C, by the way. Needless to say, I'm not gonna make the rendezvous at twenty hundred hours."

"What happened?"

He had to give Hathaway credit. The guy didn't waste time moaning and groaning when a plan went to hell. He got right to the point.

"I left the hotel early to sanitize my tail before the meeting with Zaragosa. A pair of men picked me up immediately. As soon as I made a move to shake them, they closed in and tried to off me. I ran for the emergency egress point. When I got there, the driver was dead and his boat's engine sabotaged. You know the next bit. I headed for Hollingsworth's boat."

"Did you get away clean?"

"Nope. The bastards followed me. Stole a boat and came after us."

"Us?" Hathaway asked sharply.

"Uhh, yeah. Small complication to Plan C. When I got to the *Baby Doll*, Hollingsworth's daughter was already aboard her. Which worked out pretty slick, by the way. She already had the boat untied and fired up when I got there. I jumped aboard and she took off. Probably saved my life."

"Then what?" Hathaway asked grimly.

"I exchanged fire with the hostiles while we fled."

"How's Hollingsworth's daughter?"

"Not a hair on her pretty little head out of place. She's a hell of a driver, by the way."

Hathaway replied wryly, "I'll be sure to pass your compliments on to the Congressman. Status of the shooters?"

"One down. Probably dead but not confirmed. The other's still up."

"Any idea who they were?"

"I got a half-decent look at the one who's still alive. He's a Cuban player. Guy by the name of Camarillo."

Hathaway whistled between his teeth. "Camarillo's a heavy hitter. Rumor has it he used to work directly for Fidel himself."

Mitch retorted in mock shock, "Why, sir! Fidel was a peace-loving guy. He would never stoop to violence to gain an end."

Hathaway laughed. "Save the politically correct bull for the media. You and I have both operated in Cuba and know exactly what the Old Man was capable of."

"And to think, the new regime has exponentially less scruples than he had."

Silence fell between them for a moment. Then Hathaway said, "Any idea who sent Camarillo after you? He could be freelancing these days."

Mitch turned over the concept. Fidel Castro's personal assassin cut loose to sell his skills and knowledge to anyone willing to pay? Nah. The regime in Cuba was smarter than that. They'd keep the guy on retainer. "He's not freelancing. The Cuban government had to have sent Camarillo after me."

"How did *they* find out about your meeting?"

Mitch sighed. *Aye, and there was the rub.* "How well do you know Zaragosa, sir?"

Startled silence echoed in Mitch's ear. Finally, Hathaway answered, "I've never worked with him personally. Supposedly, he's one of the CIA's best sources in Cuba. And you've got to admit, we couldn't place a mole in a much higher position if we tried."

No kidding. Zaragosa was the Deputy Prime

Minister of Cuba and widely expected to be the next *Presidente* of that tiny, but pesky nation.

A shadow crossed the hatch, and Mitch's eyes narrowed. Was Kinsey eavesdropping or harmlessly moving around the deck?

He switched to rapid Spanish. Even if she spoke the tongue, she probably wouldn't catch it at first. "Talk to me about the Congressman's daughter, sir."

Hathaway didn't miss a beat. Mitch registered yet again how good it was to work with active field operators. It cut out so much red tape and bureaucratic hemming and hawing. The navy man answered evenly, "Miss Hollingsworth has had a tough year. She caught her fiancé humping her best friend a couple weeks back and dumped him. The tabloids have had a field day with it."

That was a switch. In his experience, it was the stunning blonde who screwed around.

Hathaway continued, "Apparently the ex wasn't appreciative of the negative media coverage. To divert attention from himself, he published a series of, uhh, explicit photos of Miss Hollingsworth on the Internet."

Ouch. What a scumbag. Even spoiled little rich girls didn't deserve that.

"I expect she's looking to lie low. Blend in with the locals."

"On a hot-pink cigarette boat with her looks?" Mitch exclaimed.

Hathaway chuckled. "Any port in a storm, my friend."

Mitch thought fast. His job was to make contact with Zaragosa, infiltrate Cuba with identity papers the guy provided, then once in the country, spot any conspiracies against the guy, and protect Zaragosa's back.

Of course, having now missed the meeting with Zaragosa, that plan was shot to hell. The Cuban politician was due to return to Havana later this evening and there would be no time to arrange for a second meeting. Mitch wasn't going to get his papers today. Which meant his easy-as-pie, walk-through-the-front-door entry into Cuba was blown. Now he had to find his own way into that closed country. Illegally. Not that sneaking into Cuba posed any great challenge at the end of the day. He'd infiltrated a hell of a lot more difficult places to penetrate than Cuba in his career. But it was still a pain in the rear. Not to mention any change of plans represented a risk to the mission.

Mitch asked, "Can you guys contact Zaragosa and set up an alternate meeting with him in Cuba? Not Havana. Something on the south coast in a day or two. Maybe Cienfuegos. That's close to Zaragosa's old stomping grounds. He ought to be able to come up with an excuse to go there."

"What about you? Are *you* gonna be able to get there and blend in with the locals?"

"I've spent a fair bit of time operating in that neck of the woods. I'll be fine. Just tell Zaragosa to press on to Cuba without me and I'll hook up with him there."

Kinsey's shadow passed the porthole as she did some chore outside. Probably trying to keep busy to stave off the panic he'd seen lurking at the back of her baby blues. Odd how fate had thrust this woman into his path. Not being one to look gift horses in the mouth, however, an interesting thought struck him. He could just possibly use her looks to his advantage.

Mitch said thoughtfully, "I may have an idea of how

to get into Cuba fast. Can you scrounge up a catamaran for me? Something berthed close to Cuba."

"I'll see what I can do. I show you sailing toward the U.S. Virgin Islands right now. Is that correct?"

He glanced out the porthole. "If that means we're heading south by southwest in the middle of a whole bunch of water, that would be correct."

"I'll get the gang working on a catamaran for you."

"Not pink."

Hathaway laughed. "Roger that."

Mitch disconnected the call and pocketed the phone. He ducked through the hatch and squinted at the blazing wedge of red melting across the black water to their feet. It shrunk quickly to a narrow slash of red pulsing on the horizon.

Kinsey was already squinting at the fiery sunset. She commented over her shoulder, "Conditions are good to see the Green Flash tonight."

"The Green Flash?"

"When the sun dips below the horizon, there's an instant when its light refracts through the maximum thickness of the Earth's atmosphere and throws off the different colors of the spectrum. Sometimes you can see a flash of green. Legend says it's good luck to spot it."

Her enthusiasm was contagious. And hell, he'd take any luck he could get right about now. He squinted into the last vestiges of the setting sun. For just a second, its final rays turned a brilliant emerald green. And then they winked out. "Hey! There it was!"

She smiled over at him. "I guess that means you're gonna have good luck on this trip."

Aww, hell. The princess had dimples. They added a

little-girl charm to her bombshell looks that blew him clean away. Damn, damn, damn. He hated blondes. He didn't trust beautiful women. And he was not attracted to Kinsey Pierpont Hollingsworth!

Thankfully, his brain kicked back in before too many more seconds passed. Time to talk her into helping him. He forcibly relaxed his shoulders and shrugged, packing as much casual friendliness into his expression as he could. "For what it's worth, I work in law enforcement. I can't go into a lot of details, though."

"Do you have a badge?"

He reached for his wallet. "Sort of." He pulled out his brand, spanking-new Alcohol, Tobacco and Firearms agent ID card in the name of one Mitch Perovski, and handed it to her.

She examined it carefully, looking from the picture to him a couple times. She held the ID card out to him. "Nice picture. You're a photogenic guy."

Unaccountably, the back of his neck heated up. Every now and then someone made a comment that pierced his current legend and went all the way to the real man. It never failed to catch him off guard.

Into the suddenly awkward silence, she asked, "What brings you to the sunny Caribbean? You're a long way from home, sailor."

"Cigars."

She blinked. Frowned.

He elaborated. "Cuban cigars." The papers Zaragosa was supposed to deliver declared him to be a tobacco importer looking for new sources of fine cigars.

"Ahh. I hear they can be lucrative."

He shrugged. "A good box of Cohibas run six

hundred bucks. If your father would like a box, I'll send him some when I get home."

"He doesn't smoke," she murmured.

The conversation lagged. He didn't know what to talk about with a socialite like her. Finally, he said, "Thanks again for saving my life."

"No problem."

"I'm serious. Thank you."

"Any time," she mumbled, turning away to stare down at the navigation instruments.

The line of her neck arrested him. It was graceful. Slender. Sensuous. Wisps of hair curled at her nape underneath her short ponytail. What would happen if he breathed warmth across her skin just there? Would she cross her arms to rub away the goose bumps? Turn and melt into his arms? Kiss him into last week?

She'd kiss him right up to the part where she buried a knife in his back. He had places to go and things to do. A future president to protect. A few assassinations to commit along the way if he had to guess. Nothing out of the ordinary. He did *not* need a pampered princess like Kinsey Hollingsworth flitting around in his universe, fouling up the works and making him think thoughts he distinctly didn't want to think. First order of business: use the pretty lady to get into Cuba.

Next order of business: get rid of her.

Chapter 3

Kinsey was almost glad when darkness settled around the two of them. The rhythmic rumble of the two remaining engines soothed her—number three was running hot, and unable to find the source of the problem, she'd shut it down. The familiar salt and seaweed scent of the ocean was strong tonight. Everything about the night was magnified by the man's brooding presence beside her. Or maybe it was just her reaction to him heightening her senses to a near painful pitch. She registered his slightest movement, even a change in the depth of his breathing, every blink of his eyes, every shift in his wary gaze.

The black sky and blacker sea merged into a single great expanse, a beast that had swallowed them whole. Normally, she loved this magnificent solitude. But tonight her soul was turbulent, disturbed by the leashed energy of the stranger beside her.

Reluctantly, she turned on the instrument back lighting. Its red glow intruded into the sensual mystery of the dark, breaking the spell.

"Head for the nearest inhabited island at our best forward speed."

He was back to orders and demands, this hard man. Nothing compromising or yielding about him.

She scanned the horizon and made out a faint black hump in the distance, a few lights twinkling along its spine. "There's the north coast of St. Thomas now," she replied.

"Find us somewhere to put ashore where we can hide this garish boat. Whatever possessed your father to paint it peppermint-pink, anyway?"

Kinsey rolled her eyes. "The trophy wife."

"I beg your pardon?"

"My father traded in my mother when she hit fifty for a new model. Giselle is twenty-eight now."

"Isn't that about how old you are?"

"Yeah. How creepy is that? But hey, she's gotten three *Vogue* covers and looks great on television."

Mitch sounded almost bitter when he commented, "I learned a long time ago not to put any stock in a woman's looks."

Wow. Definite raw nerve there. She changed the subject quickly. "If you want to hide this monster, we'll need to get her under a roof. There's a big marina near Frenchtown with some covered slips, but it's right by where the cruise ships come in. People crawl all over that area. Maybe something private..." She ran through the list of who she knew on the island. "I've got it. A sorority sister of mine and her husband have a place in Magen's Bay. And I think they have a boathouse."

A cynical look passed across his features. "Of course they do."

What was his problem? She shrugged and pointed the *Baby Doll* toward Magen's Bay. Only about half the estates lining its very exclusive, very private shores were lit tonight. Summer wasn't prime season for Caribbean vacation homes. She had a little trouble finding the right mansion, but eventually spotted it high above the water. Its windows were dark.

"Looks like nobody's home," she commented.

"Think they'll mind if we help ourselves to the boathouse?" Mitch murmured.

"No. We go way back. They'll understand."

"How do you know these people's boathouse will have an empty slip?"

She shrugged. "They always move their yacht up to Hyannis for the summer."

"Right. Hyannis."

She glanced over at him. "Look, I can't help it if I know some rich people. Mitzi and her husband are actually very nice."

"It's not the rich part I object to. It's the spoiled part."

She cut the engine and let the *Baby Doll* drift toward the boathouse. "Are you calling me spoiled?"

"If the shoe fits."

"The shoe does *not* fit. I can't help being born into a wealthy family." He was doing the same thing everyone else did. They took one look at her, labeled her a spoiled little rich girl and completely wrote her off as a waste of oxygen on the planet. What was it going to take for someone to take her seriously?

Gritting her teeth in frustration, she guided the *Baby Doll* to the dock and Mitch jumped ashore. He made his way to the locked boathouse doors and did something to them that didn't take more than a few seconds. And then they swung open. She eased the *Baby Doll* into the empty slip and tossed him a line. While he tied off the prow, she shut down the engines and tied off the aft line.

In the abrupt silence inside the barnlike structure, a thick blanket of darkness wrapped around them, as warm and sultry as the night without.

"What jobs have you ever held?" he challenged.

Still grinding that axe, was he? "I graduated with honors in English from Vassar and was an intern in my father's law firm. And I was a darned good one, too."

He shook his head, a sharp movement in the dark. "Not a paying job, and you were working for daddy. Nobody was going to bust your chops or fire you from that place. Name me one real job you've ever had."

She huffed in irritation.

"I rest my case," he stated archly.

Annoyed, she replied, "How many charity balls for thousands of guests have you organized from scratch? How many millions of dollars have you raised for worthy causes and given away? How many scholarships have you interviewed a hundred people for and then granted? How many press conferences have you endured? How many political campaigns have you spent a year working on around the clock, road tripping and stumping and getting by on two and three hours of sleep a night for months on end?"

He threw up his hands in mock surrender. "All right, all right. So you don't sit around on daddy's fancy boat every day working on your perfect tan." But he still didn't sound convinced.

She wasn't quite sure why, but it was tremendously important to her that this supremely competent man perceive her as being able to do something worthwhile. Maybe she was sick of being compared to tabloid princesses. Or maybe it was because she'd felt so helpless in the face of being shot at. He, on the other hand, had taken action. He shot back. He took out his enemies. And she...she splashed some water at them with her cute pink boat.

Chad slept with her best friend and then posted those damned pictures of her on the Internet when she dared to be mad about him sleeping with her maid of honor two weeks before their wedding. And all she'd managed to do was tuck her tail and run away. She wished she had a gun like Mitch's. She'd have blown off both their heads with it. Okay. Maybe not shot them. But she'd have scared them both to death. But no. She'd been as weak and spineless, as *useless,* as Mitch thought she was. Her face burned with the humiliation of it all.

She *was* useful, dammit! Just because her entire family and everyone she knew thought she was supposed to spend her life doing nothing more than being attractive fluff to decorate the arm of some powerful successful man, didn't mean it was true.

She finished buttoning up the *Baby Doll* for the night, her movements a little too jerky. Mitch prowled a circuit around both the outside and inside of the boathouse and finally came to a halt beside the boat. His gaze was black. Inscrutable in the near-total darkness.

"Now what?" she grumbled, still miffed.

"Now I make a phone call. And we sit tight until the cavalry comes for us."

She watched as he pulled out his cell phone.

"It's me," he muttered into it. "St. Thomas. In a boathouse at some private estate on Magen's Bay. Heh, swanky doesn't quite cover it. Any luck on a catamaran?"

A short pause while he listened to whomever he was talking with. She could swear his eyes glowed in the dark, gold and dangerous. It must be a trick of the faint moonlight creeping in through the boathouse windows, but the effect was eerie.

Without warning, his gaze speared into her, pinning her in place. "I'm telling you, she can do it. She's perfect for it." A short pause. "Yes, I know the risks. And yes, I'm sure."

He sounded like he was trying to convince himself as much as the person on the other end of the line about whatever they were talking about.

"Okay. Call me back." He disconnected.

Not long on words, her pantherlike companion. When he didn't say anything to her after he pocketed the phone, she said, "And?"

"And we stay here while my people set up transportation for us."

"To where?"

He didn't answer right away. In fact, he almost looked hesitant to tell her. How bad could it be? He'd need to take her someplace secluded, far away from Cuba where the killer wouldn't think to look for her. Maybe Europe. It was nice there at this time of year.

"How do you feel about big game hunting?" he asked.

"Africa?" she blurted, surprised, "It's awfully hot there at this time of year. But I suppose I'm up for a safari. As long as we don't shoot anything. But I could go for some big game photography." Now that she thought about it, she could see where he'd feel at home on the Dark Continent.

"Not Africa," he bit out.

"Then where?"

Finally, he said reluctantly, "Cuba."

"What?" she squawked. "But that's where your assassin is from."

"That's correct. It'll just be for a few days. Long enough for me to find our guy and neutralize him. His name's Camarillo, by the way."

"We need to stay away from him. He'll try to kill us again!"

"That's why we're going to hunt him down and eliminate him before he gets us. Ops thinks it would be safer to go on the offensive and not sit back and wait for him to come to us."

Shock rendered her speechless. They were going hunting for their would-be killer? She burst out, "That's the dumbest idea I've ever heard of."

He snorted without humor. "Wait till you get a load of the next part, where you act as my cover to smuggle me into Cuba."

"How am I supposed to do that?"

"Can you handle a sailboat as well as you handle a motorboat?"

"Well, yes." She frowned. "How did you know that?"

He made a noise that might pass in some circles for a laugh. "Tortola? Hyannis? Magen's Bay? You grew up on water. And where there are rich people and water, there are sailboats."

"I happen to prefer motorboats," she replied a little stiffly. She hated fitting his stereotype of her, but she had, in fact, grown up around boats of all kinds.

Mitch's voice rasped across her skin like a cat's rough tongue, drawing her attention once more. "I need you to sail a wounded catamaran into port on the south side of Cuba and request repairs. They'll let you come ashore in an emergency. I'm going to hide in one of the pontoons. Once you've docked, I'll sneak out and we'll head inland from there."

"Sounds dangerous."

"Not especially. If the Cubans catch us, they'll only throw us into prison. In six months, a year tops, the U.S. government will negotiate our release. I figure with your father being who he is, the Cubans will spring us after a few weeks. At least, they'll spring *you* that fast."

"I do not want to be incarcerated in a Cuban jail, thank you very much."

"Me, neither. That's why you're going to pay attention and do what I tell you to."

"I don't like it," she announced.

"Neither do I. But I've got no time to fool around with setting up another entry into Cuba. You're it, Miss Hollingsworth. We need to stick together anyway until I kill Camarillo. I may as well put you to some good use."

"Gee, thanks. I always love sounding like some sort of disposable power tool."

"You don't throw out power tools," he corrected gently.

She merely narrowed her eyes and glared at him. Fine. So she'd never seen a power tool in person in her life. He knew darn good and well what she had meant. She sulked for several minutes, trying to figure out some better way to get into Cuba. But she was completely out of her league on this one. She turned her attention to something that had bothered her from the very beginning. "How did Camarillo find you? Wasn't your meeting with whoever you were supposed to meet with a secret?"

He looked roundly irritated that she dared to question his work and didn't bother to answer.

She wasn't about to let him go all strong and silent on her, like she didn't matter enough to talk to. No, sirree. She got enough of that from her father. She poked again—something simple to get him talking. "How did you get those boathouse doors open?"

His teeth flashed white in the darkness. "Have you ever heard of a don't ask, don't tell policy? If you won't ask, I won't tell."

She absorbed that one in silence. Eventually, she asked, "How long are we supposed to sit here, waiting for your phone call?"

He shrugged. "Could be all night."

Great. All night in a dark, secluded place with this macho male. Darned if that didn't make her heart beat a little faster. More in an attempt to distract herself than actually make conversation, she commented lightly, "I don't know about you, but I'm hungry."

"Gee, I'll just call the local French gourmet delivery joint and have them bring us a seven-course meal," he retorted.

She glared and replied loftily, "There's food in the *Baby Doll*'s galley."

He looked startled, like he'd forgotten for a moment

that the *Baby Doll* had a compact, but completely stocked, cabin.

She ducked below and turned on the halogen track lighting. It twinkled subtly overhead, lending the space a romantic glow. She opened the small cupboard above the microwave oven. "There's canned spaghetti or tuna fish," she called up.

"I'll take spaghetti." He joined her in the tiny cabin, filling its entire space with his dark presence. He sprawled on the leather couch, a feline predator at rest. She passed him a piping hot container of spaghetti and zapped one for herself. When it was ready, she moved to the far end of the couch and perched cautiously on it. She promptly burned her tongue, but did her best not to show it. Darn, that man flustered her! She shifted uncomfortably in her seat.

"We could always break into the main house and raid the pantry," he suggested.

"Let's not," Kinsey said dryly. "We're already imposing. And these are my friends."

His only reply was a casual shrug.

They finished their meal, such as it was, in silence. Mitch arose and held out his hand for her cup and spoon. She handed them over and he tossed them in the galley's sink. He'd just turned to head for the steps when his cell phone shattered the deep silence. Kinsey jumped nearly as hard as he did. He fished it out of his pocket.

"Go," he bit out.

His eyebrows drew together in a frown as he listened, and his gaze flicked over to her. Whoever was on the other end of the conversation was talking about her, she was sure of it.

"I'll see what I can do," Mitch rumbled. He disconnected. Turned to face her. "Seems we've got a little problem. Your father doesn't want you to help us with this operation. He thinks it'll place you in too much danger. You're, and I quote, totally unprepared to deal with the pressures of the situation."

Heat flooded her face. This was exactly what she was talking about! People took one look at her and assumed she wasn't good for anything. "In other words, he thinks I can't hack it," she forced out.

"More or less."

"Give me your phone," she snapped. She held out her open palm expectantly. One eyebrow raised, he laid the device in her hand.

She stabbed out her father's private number and waited impatiently for the call to go through. Richard Hollingsworth's voice came on the line. "Hello?"

"Hi Dad, it's your useless, spoiled daughter calling."

"Honey, are you all right? They told me some guy shot at you today."

"Oh, I'm fine. And that guy's shark bait," she replied breezily. "The man who saved my life today needs a favor from me, though, and I'm going to do it. I hear you're worried, so I'm calling to tell you I'll be fine. He says I need to stay with him and I believe him. I trust this man implicitly to keep me safe."

Mitch's gaze riveted on her at those words. Her embarrassed gaze skittered away from his.

"Kinsey, do you have any idea who this Perovski fellow is? I had my staff run a profile on him, and you can't believe some of the things he's done. Plainly put, he's a killer. He's a covert operator and runs around blowing things up and assassinating people for a living. You have no business being around someone like him."

The condescension in her father's voice set her teeth on edge. "Be that as it may, I'm going to help him with the next phase of his current mission."

"No."

"I wasn't calling to ask permission, Dad. I'm telling you how it's going to be."

Her father's voice rose to a bull roar. "Don't you take that tone with me, young lady. I control your trust fund. And I forbid you to do this."

"I'm sorry you feel that way. But I am going to do it."

"I'll cut you off. No money, no credit cards, no bank account. Nothing."

Twenty minutes ago, that threat might have given her pause. But after Mitch's scathing opinion of her utter uselessness as a human being, she'd be damned if her father would bully her out of this.

"Do what you have to, Dad, but my decision's made. Good night." She closed the phone and handed it back to Mitch in silence.

"What did he threaten to do to you?" Mitch asked quietly.

"He's cutting me off financially."

"Totally?" Mitch sounded surprised.

"Yup."

"Man, that sucks. I can look into having the boys put you on the payroll for the duration of this op if you'd like."

She grinned ruefully. "Thanks, but I'll muddle through until he gets over his snit. My mother is loaded, compliments of her divorce lawyer, and she'll slip me some cash if I empty my bank account before he gets over his snit. Besides, I can always threaten to go public with what my father's doing to me and he'll back off. Negative publicity is very bad for a man in his position. He's up for reelection this November."

Mitch winced and grinned simultaneously. "Ouch. Blackmailing your old man? That's cold. I like it."

She grinned back, reassured she'd made the right decision. She wanted some of the competence that was Mitch Perovski for herself. If she spent a few days with him, maybe some of that cool confidence of his would rub off on her. Goodness knew, she needed it. If he could show her how to get people to take her even a little more seriously, it would be worth all the money in her trust fund and more. She was sick and tired of being walked all over.

In fact, the more she thought about it, the more she liked the idea. If she could shed her socialite image and become a strong, independent woman...oh, yes. The idea made her tingle from head to toe. Wild horses weren't going to keep her away from Mitch Perovski, no matter what risk that entailed.

Chapter 4

Mitch glanced around the tight confines of the *Baby Doll*'s cabin. The sofa no doubt folded out into a bed. One bed. Two people. He winced mentally. He could be a gentleman and offer to sleep up top, propped up in one of the chairs or stretched out on the hard deck. But this was likely to be the last decent night's sleep he got for the next several months, and dammit, they were both adults. They could sleep in the same bed without anything untoward happening between them.

Kinsey stifled a yawn.

He said lightly, "Let's get some shut-eye. No telling when the boys will be here to pick us up. Operations rule number one: sleep when you can."

She nodded without protest, unlocked the sofa, and pulled it out into a bed. With her working at one end and him at the other, they made the bed with satin sheets—

what else for the *Baby Doll?*—cashmere blankets, and fluffy eiderdown pillows.

"Where are you sleeping?" she asked, all innocence.

"Here. How about you?"

Her alarmed blue gaze snapped to his. She looked down at the inviting bed. Back up at him. "Oh."

He shrugged, but it didn't relieve the abrupt tension in his shoulders. "I don't know about you, but I'm beat. And tomorrow promises to be rougher than today." Why did he give a damn if she refused to sleep with him or not? She wasn't some princess—which she was taking great pains to convince him of. She was just a person. Just like him.

Dammit, not just like him. She lived in the lap of luxury, in a world of yachts and mansions and summers in Hyannis. They were as different as day and night. And he'd do well to remember that. He'd use her to get into Cuba, he'd kill Camarillo before the bastard could kill her, thereby sending a powerful message to Camarillo's comrades that Kinsey Hollingsworth was off limits. And then they'd each get on with their regularly scheduled lives. He'd go back to being a sewer rat, and she'd go back to doing whatever she did, hopefully unmolested. Tanning on sleek cigarette boats in a thousand-dollar bikini.

"You take the side by the hull," he directed. "I'll sleep closest to the hatch."

She lurched. "Do you think Camarillo might find us here?"

"Not a chance. He wouldn't look for me in a place like this in a thousand years." And that was why she was going to be such a great cover to get him into Cuba.

Nobody in their right mind would look at her and see a covert operative running a scam.

She crawled under the covers and scooted to the far side of the bed, plastered against the wall. He turned off the lights and, under cover of darkness, tucked his pistol under his pillow. He sat down on the edge of the bed and thought he heard her squirm even farther away from him

"I won't bite," he growled.

"I'm not so sure about that," she retorted.

He grinned into the dark. If she only knew. He'd bet he could bite her so he'd have her begging him for more in under five minutes. Hell, two minutes.

"Sweet dreams, Mitch."

Right. Like there was anything sweet about his dreams. Not after the life he'd lived. "You, too."

He stretched out on possibly the most comfortable mattress he'd ever experienced. One of those memory foam things that contoured itself to fit his body to perfection. Some mission this was starting out to be. Here he was in the perfect bed—hell, the thing was even adorned with a blond bombshell—and all he could do was lie still, teeth gritted, and pray for the night to be over.

Kinsey's breathing lightened into the gentle rhythm of sleep more quickly than he expected. The gunfight earlier must've really taken the starch out of her. But then it occurred to him that her rapid sleep also meant she trusted him. How had she described it to her old man? She trusted him implicitly with her life? Ahh, if only she knew. If she had any idea of the thoughts of her dancing across his mind's eye right now, she'd run screaming from him.

Not that he meant anything by it. Stripping her naked in his mind was just an idle fancy to pass the time and distract him from his insomnia. He certainly wasn't about to act on it. She was a resource for a mission and emphatically not his sort of female. At least not anymore. As soon as she got him into Cuba, he'd send her home to daddy and a raft of expensive, private bodyguards. And that was *not* a pang of regret stabbing his gut, dammit!

He must've drifted to sleep, because some time later, he jerked awake abruptly. He froze, listening. What had wakened him? The night sounds of St. Thomas were mostly silent, a few crickets and frogs the only remaining chorus outside. The *Baby Doll* rocked ever so faintly beneath him, so soothing he was half-asleep again already.

Kinsey gave a faint start beside him and made a frightened sound. Aww, crap. She was having a nightmare. This was his cue to roll over and gather her into his arms and comfort her. Except he didn't want to put his hands on her, didn't want to press her against him. Women like her were poison. He'd just as soon hug a rattlesnake.

She jerked again, her breathing fast and hard. She half sat up, then collapsed back against her pillow.

"You all right?" he asked gruffly.

"I had a bad dream."

"Let me guess. It involved Cuban guys with giant guns chasing you."

"Something like that."

"Shrug it off. A nightmare is just your mind's way of blowing off some steam after a traumatic event. It doesn't mean anything."

"Right." A pause. Then her voice came out of the dark, faintly sarcastic. "Thanks for the comforting advice. I'll never fear another nightmare again as long as I live."

"Look. I don't do the whole touchy-feely thing. I'll stomp all over your emotions in the middle of an op and not think twice about it. I'm a bastard. The sooner you realize that, the better we'll get along."

Hurt silence was her only response to that salvo. Damn. He really was a bastard.

He thought she'd already gone back to sleep when her voice drifted out of the dark. "Then why are you insisting on protecting me until Camarillo's dead?"

"Because it's the right thing to do," he bit out.

"A real bastard wouldn't care enough about someone else to do the right thing. You're a grouch. But not a bastard."

"Thank you…I think," he retorted.

"You're welcome," she replied lightly.

"Go to sleep."

"Yes sir, Mr. Grouch, sir."

A smile twitched at the corners of his mouth. How did she do that? She'd turned aside his irritation effortlessly. Alarm coursed through him. What had he done, saddling himself with this woman for days, or even weeks?

Kinsey went back to sleep with a smile on her lips and woke up with one on them in the morning…if the first hint of dawn could rightly be called morning. The sky in the east was pink, but the sun hadn't risen above the verdant mountains ringing Magen's Bay when Mitch touched her arm lightly. At the brush of his fingers against her skin, she popped wide awake.

He looked even rougher and more dangerous this morning with a stubble of beard darkening his jaw. "It's time to go."

She sat up abruptly, the covers pooling around her waist. His gaze dropped to her chest for an instant, but then jerked away as quickly. She was startled to find herself relieved at the brief verification that a red-blooded male actually did live inside the cold predator. She crawled on her hands and knees across the wide bed and swung her bare feet to the cold floor.

"I wish I had some real clothes," she remarked wistfully. "I'm going to get plenty sick of this bikini and T-shirt in the next week or two."

"I'm sure the folks at the Bat Cave can arrange for some real clothes. Maybe not the designer labels you're used to, but clothes."

"Would you get off your high horse about my financial background?"

"It's hard to forget with you looking the way you do."

She glared at him. "Whatever's left of yesterday's mascara is probably smeared all over my face by now. I undoubtedly have a bad case of bed head, and I haven't had a shower in twenty-four hours. I'm wearing a junky T-shirt and not a whole lot more. I look like hell, and I know it. So cut the crap about my looks."

He crossed his arms, his expression black. His molten gaze raked down her person, far too slowly and thoroughly, all the way to her pedicured toes and back up to her eyes. To say she felt stripped naked didn't quite cover it. She felt…invaded. And caressed. And, oh my, appreciated in a very, very female way.

"Honey, if that's as bad as it ever gets with you, I'd

hate to see you gussied up. You look like a top-drawer princess just as you are."

She frowned. How did he manage to make such a lavish compliment sound like such an insult? A strange sound intruded upon her ruminations. A distant, heavy thumping. She lurched in surprise and bumped into Mitch.

"What's that?" she gasped.

Mitch turned quickly and took all three steps up onto deck in a single, athletic bound. "Stay here," he ordered as a pistol materialized in his hand.

She briefly considered hiding in the closet-size bathroom, but decided any bad guy would search there right away.

"You can come out, Kinsey. It's the H.O.T. Watch."

The H.O.T. Watch? He mentioned that before. Sounded like a bunch of comic-book heroes. Cautiously, she went up onto deck. Three male silhouettes filled the boathouse doors. She recognized Mitch's sleek, powerful outline right away. He lifted a hand and gestured her to come over to him.

He was deep in conversation with another man in rapid Spanish she couldn't entirely follow. Strange, because she actually spoke the language reasonably well. They were using specialized vocabulary she only vaguely recognized as dealing with weapons of some kind. She moved to his side, and was startled when he absently reached out and looped an arm about her shoulders, pulling her close to him.

Oh yes. Entirely male. Powerful, protective, alpha male. It was really quite nice to cuddle up to all that brawn.

Eventually there was a break in the discussion.

"This is Kinsey," Mitch said to the first man.

"I'm Brady. Nice to meet you, ma'am."

Was that his first name or last name? He didn't look like the kind of guy she could ask the question of readily. He had to be military with that short hair and ramrod-straight bearing. And then there was the whole ma'am thing. The other guy was introduced as Captain Scott Cash. His dancing green eyes were much more inviting than the first man's.

To him, she commented, "You get harassed about your name and rank a lot, don't you?"

He grinned back at her. "Wait until I become Major Cash."

Mitch interrupted sharply, "Ready to go?"

She looked up into his scowling visage. "Well, I've got a ton of stuff to pack. It'll take hours before I'm ready."

"Very funny. Let's move out, gentlemen."

His big hand wrapped around her elbow and he steered her out the door with easy strength. She felt like a panther cub with its mother's jaws around her neck, carrying her to safety. Mitch's touch was gentle, but unmistakably powerful. The other men fell in behind her and Mitch as they stepped outside the boathouse. A chunky helicopter sat in the mansion's back yard, its rotors spinning and a pair of helmeted pilots sitting at the controls. The paint job was blue-gray on the bottom and green on the top.

Mitch hustled her up the stone steps from the beach to the wide lawn and urged her into a jog when they reached the manicured grass. She couldn't help crouching low as they moved under the rotor blades. A wide door swung open in front of them, and Mitch helped her inside.

She sat down on a hard seat and looked around for a seat belt. She started when Mitch crouched in front of her and plunged both hands behind her hips. His palms cupped her derriere and she'd have bolted out of the seat if that wouldn't have flung her straight into his arms.

Their gazes met, hers wide with shock, his narrow with irritation. He yanked his hands back roughly, bringing with them the halves of her seat belt. He guided a pair of shoulder straps over both of her breasts, the wide nylon blatantly rubbing the sensitive flesh they were smashing. His hands came together in her lap and she grew possibly more shocked. His nimble fingers fumbled embarrassingly close to the junction of her thighs, and then his hands lifted away. She looked down. Her seat belt was a five-point affair with a round buckle sitting low on her belly. Thankfully the shoulder straps hid the way her nipples had hardened under her thin T-shirt at his touch.

"Are you done?" she muttered.

His blazing gaze caught hers. "I haven't even gotten started yet," he growled back.

She gulped as he slid into the seat across from her and buckled his own safety harness. Scott Cash sat on her right, and the enigmatic Brady took a seat beside Mitch. Two crew members took the remaining seats. As soon as one of them slid the big door shut, the bird lifted off the ground, swooping forward fast and then banking into a steep, accelerating turn.

"Where are we going?" she shouted over the noise to Mitch.

"It'll take a couple hours to get there," he shouted back. "If you want to take a nap, go ahead. I know you slept lousy last night."

And how did he know that? Other than the nightmare that had woken her up so abruptly, of course. She didn't want to ask in front of the other men, so she just glared at him for being rude enough to comment on it. He stared back at her implacably. Every now and then a jostle of the helicopter sent his knees banging into hers. At some point, he stretched his powerful legs out, his feet extending all the way under her seat. The pose forced her legs apart so his calves could slip between hers. It was intimate and aggressive. Like the man.

And yet, he'd declined to touch her last night, even when she'd needed and wanted a hug from him. Was he truly the bastard he claimed to be, or was there more to it than that? She studied him, his eyes closed, his arms crossed over his chest in an eye-catching display of bulging biceps. She'd been around plenty of men who were intimidated by her beauty and hesitated to touch her. Was that it? Was he actually attracted enough to her to be shy?

Mitch Perovski shy? The thought made her smile.

"What?" he bit out.

She started. How had he seen her smile? His eyes were closed. "I beg your pardon?"

"What are you grinning about like that?"

Her smile returned, wider than before. "Nothing. Nothing at all."

He humphed, recrossed his arms over his chest, and closed his eyes once more. Whether or not he actually slept, she couldn't tell. But she eventually followed suit and let the rotor wash and jet noise coax her heavy eyelids closed. What was that thing he'd said last night about sleeping when she could? She took his advice and drifted off.

* * *

"Wake up, Kinsey."

She jolted to consciousness. The helicopter was still vibrating, thumping loudly around her. Mitch was leaning forward, his hand resting on her bare knee. Darned if heat wasn't shooting straight up the inside of her thigh to her nether regions. She drew in a quick breath of surprise. His all too perceptive eyes flashed in male satisfaction for the barest instant before he released her leg and leaned back, resuming his negligent, feline sprawl.

"Where are we?" she asked sleepily.

"Almost there."

She didn't even bother to ask where "there" was. If he'd wanted to tell her, he would have. She sighed. "How long was I asleep?"

"Three hours."

Wow. How fast could a helicopter go, anyway? Maybe two hundred miles per hour? That meant they could be anywhere up to six hundred miles away from St. Thomas. That encompassed a pretty big chunk of the eastern Caribbean.

The helicopter dropped alarmingly and she clutched at the nearest thing, which turned out to be Scott Cash's rock-hard forearm. "What was that?" she blurted.

Mitch scowled pointedly at her hand on the other man's arm. "We're coming in for a landing. Nothing to panic over."

She released the captain's arm with a smile of gratitude and apology. At least he was smiling back at her. Broadly. With dimples.

Mitch regained her attention abruptly by announcing, "Time to put the blindfold on you."

"What for?"

He shrugged. "Secret location. You're not allowed to see anything that might let you identify it later."

"You're kidding." Bat caves? Secret locations? This was definitely turning into a comic book.

He leaned forward with a black, cloth blindfold like an airplane passenger might wear to sleep in flight. He placed it over her eyes, then slipped the elastic strap behind her head. He gathered her hair in a rough ponytail, his fingertips caressing the nape of her neck and sending shivers shooting all the way to her toes. He pulled her hair through the elastic strap and released it in a cascade of silken softness against her skin. Goose bumps erupted on her arms, and damned if he didn't notice and grin.

"Can you see anything?" he asked.

"Like I'd tell you if I could?" she retorted. Cash chuckled beside her. She felt Mitch's scowl without any need to see it. His fingers skimmed all the way around the edge of the mask, checking the seal, and incidentally unleashing a horde of butterflies in her stomach. He was messing with her on purpose. Was he just trying to make her uncomfortable, or was he getting a kick out of her involuntary reactions to him? Or maybe he was testing her reactions to him for some other reason altogether. One that had to do with the way his eyes glowed whenever he looked at her.

The helicopter thudded gently to the ground. In a few moments the engines cut, and the thwocking of the rotor blades slowed rapidly.

"Okay, out we go," Mitch muttered. His hand fumbled at her lap belt and her breath hitched far too revealingly for her comfort. Just as well she couldn't see him. His strong hands guided her outside. A little light leaked around the edges of the mask, and the sun warmed her skin. She heard and smelled the ocean nearby and sand gave way underfoot. A beach, then.

"This way," Mitch murmured. His hand slid under her elbow, and his big body rubbed lightly against her side. She was surprised at how horribly disoriented she became in a matter of moments. She leaned closer to Mitch, intensely disliking this sudden vulnerability. And yet, of all the men she'd ever met, she had the most confidence in him to keep her safe. After his lethal display of skills yesterday, she had faith he was one of the deadliest people around. Although frankly, his buddies hadn't looked much less dangerous.

After maybe a hundred strides through more sand, she heard a door open in front of her.

"Steps downward," he murmured.

She felt with her foot, stumbling a bit on the first step. But Mitch's arm snaked around her waist, catching her and steadying her. Of course, it also plastered her against his side. Sensations of his body against hers slammed into her. Hard muscle. Lean waist. Hot. Vibrant. Powerful. Oh so very male.

He cleared his throat and carefully set her away from him. She looped her left hand under his elbow once more. She stuck out her right hand for balance and encountered a cool, rough wall. *Stone.* The steps, while individually fairly shallow, went on forever. She lost count of them somewhere in the seventies.

And then, without warning, her foot reached out for another step and ran into level floor. It was hard and smooth like concrete. The air currents around her shifted and the echo of their feet changed as if they'd stepped out into an open space.

Mitch stopped with her huddled close to him. She heard some metallic clanking and an odd hissing noise. Then he urged her forward with a solicitous hand in the small of her back. "Careful now. This is a big step. You'll have to bend down. Grab that metal bar right there. Now swing your right leg out and down."

What in the world? It felt like she was climbing down into something. As she put weight on her right foot, the surface beneath her gave slightly. Ahh. A boat. She frowned under the mask. A boat underground? What was this?

She stumbled forward a few more steps and then Mitch guided her down into a comfortable, cushioned seat. Her ears popped like the space around her had pressurized and her frown deepened. "What is this?" she demanded. "Where am I?"

"You're aboard a submarine. Not too much longer, now, and you can take off your blindfold."

A *submarine?* Good grief. Sure enough, a low rumble started under her feet, and her seat began to sway gently. They must have motored forward and down for ten or fifteen minutes, and then the blindfold suddenly lifted away from her eyes.

She blinked around in the red-lit semidark. She was, indeed, on a minisub. A small, thick window at her left looked out on a mostly dark ocean. They were deep, then. From her experience with scuba diving, she'd estimate they were well over a hundred feet down. Momentary claustrophobia tightened her chest. So much water pressing down on top of them. The weight of it could crush them if this vessel failed.

"Where in the world are we going?" she asked Mitch, who sat across from her again.

"H.O.T. Watch headquarters. We've got to pick up some gear before we head into Cuba, and I need a last-minute intelligence briefing before we make our run." He glanced down at her unclad legs. "And we've got to get you some clothes. I'm not going to be able to concentrate if I have to keep looking at your legs all the time."

"What's wrong with my legs?" She'd just had them waxed, and she had a pretty good tan going if she said so herself. Her limbs were long and toned and sleek. She'd always thought of them as one of her best assets.

"Nothing's wrong with your legs," he grumbled. "That's the problem."

Captain Cash piped up from her right. "Hark. Is Lancer actually showing signs of being human after all?"

Lancer? Was that some sort of nickname of his? It was a good name for him. Sharp. Lethal. Something that drew blood.

Mitch scowled at his comrade. "Shut up, Scottie."

Brady laughed. "I think you're right, Scott. The guy's human after all. Thanks for answering that question for us, Miss Hollingsworth."

She crossed one slender leg over the other, dangling her flip-flop from her toes in Mitch's direction. "My pleasure," she drawled at Brady. For good measure, she crossed her arms, pushing up her chest under her T-shirt. Too bad she had the shirt over her bikini top. Nonetheless, Mitch's gaze dropped involuntarily to the sudden curves. When it lifted again to hers, as brilliant and turbulent as the surface of the sun, she smirked back at him.

He crossed his own arms and turned a shoulder to her, staring fixedly out the window.

Triumph surged in her breast. She glanced over at Brady. "How long is this little joy ride going to take?"

He shrugged. "A while."

"Why all this secrecy?"

Brady replied, "The facility we're going to is highly classified. Only a handful of people know it exists, let alone where it is. The only reason you get to go there is because time is of the essence and who your father is. It's as much for your protection as ours that we're concealing its location from you."

"Seems like you're going to an awful lot of trouble. You could always just ask me to promise not to tell where it is. I'd give you my word on it, you know."

Mitch interjected, saying harshly, "And when you're taken prisoner and tortured for the information, how long do you think you could hold out?"

She jerked back, stung. The rest of the ride, which lasted upward of an hour, finished in silence, stony from him and irritated from her. At one point, she caught Brady looking back and forth between the two of them in quiet amusement, like he thought they were perfect for each other. Whatever. Mitch Perovski was a jerk. She would prove to him that she was no dimwit socialite and smuggle his happy butt into Cuba, but then she was done with him.

Chapter 5

Mitch watched as the submarine ducked under a black overhang of rock, skimming close enough to it to make Kinsey gasp. He'd taken this ride a number of times and that spot never failed to make him hold his breath. There was a surface entrance to the Bat Cave, but because of its vulnerability to attack, *nobody* but H.O.T. Watch staff knew its location.

The sub slowed and came to a stop. Kinsey leaned forward to peer out the window, but Mitch knew she'd see nothing but blackness. The pilot was centering the vessel below a vertical tube formed eons ago by upwelling magma. The sub would begin an elevator-like ascent up the tube momentarily. Sure enough, the vessel lurched gently beneath his feet and began to rise.

Kinsey glanced over at him for reassurance. He spared her a single nod to indicate that everything was okay. He kept trying to distance himself from her, to achieve cold, calm detachment from his temporary partner. But every time she succumbed to a moment of vulnerability, his protective instincts roared to the fore and there wasn't a damned thing he could do about it.

"Are you going to blindfold me when we get off this thing?" Kinsey asked, her musical voice wavering slightly.

Dammit, she was doing it again. He couldn't help the gentleness that crept into his voice. "No. We'll be underground. You won't be able to see any identifying features that might give away where we are."

She lapsed into apprehensive silence. Her blue eyes were big and dark, almost childlike, making her look like a girl-woman in a siren's body. Like it or not, she was beautiful. And he wanted her. Compared to Janine—the woman who'd put him off leggy blondes and their treacherous hearts in the first place—Kinsey was a diamond to Janine's lump of coal. Janine had been pretty, but Kinsey was gorgeous. Janine had been tall and leggy, as was Kinsey—but Kinsey also moved with the unconscious grace of a dancer. Janine knew she was hot and flaunted it. Kinsey didn't need to have everyone in a room looking at her. Which, of course, had exactly the opposite effect.

Regardless, he wasn't about to trust Kinsey's heart for a second. Women as beautiful as she was didn't wait around for men who disappeared for months at a time, mostly unable to communicate with their women while undercover. Janine sure as hell hadn't waited around for him. Who knew how long she'd fooled around on him before she came up pregnant, months after he could possibly have been the father. The hell of it was he still supported the boy. But dammit, he couldn't abandon a baby to Janine's erratic finances. Not even some other guy's kid.

The pilot's voice announcing that they were clear to open hatches startled Mitch out of his grim thoughts.

As he helped Kinsey climb out of the vessel, she murmured, "Are you all right?"

"Why do you ask?"

"You look like you're headed to your own execution."

He smiled reluctantly. "I was just ruminating on what a bastard I am."

She replied sympathetically, "No wonder you look so depressed."

A snort of laughter escaped him before he even felt it coming. He slipped a hand under her elbow, relishing the slide of tender flesh under the pad of his thumb, and helped her off the sub. She glanced up to smile her thanks at him, and their gazes met and held for a moment before hers slid away shyly.

Possessiveness roared through him, and he wrestled unsuccessfully with the sensation as Scott Cash led the way upstairs to the main facility. He actually had to bite back a protest when Jennifer Blackfoot took Kinsey in hand and whisked her away to the bowels of the Bat Cave to brief and, hopefully, scrounge up some clothes for her. Off balance, he headed for the infirmary with Hathaway in tow. The fastest way to the compact first aid facility was through the ops center.

He stepped out onto the main floor and experienced the surreal sensation of having stepped into a science fiction movie. The huge space, hollowed out of an extinct volcano, could easily hold a football field. The broad floor was crammed with the latest electronics and surveillance equipment on the planet today. At least two dozen technicians manned the consoles and banks of computers. His favorite feature of the room by far, though, was the twenty-foot tall wall of digital screens currently displaying maps of the world and the Caribbean. Definite sci-fi movie material. A few of the technicians looked up to greet him as he passed through, en route.

As a technician efficiently unwrapped his clumsy bandage and commenced cleaning the wound on his shoulder, Hathaway closed the door and moved around to stand in front of him.

"What's the status of Miss Hollingsworth? Is she in or out on this mission?"

"She's in."

Hathaway made a face. "Her old man's gonna have a fit. "

"She has already discussed it with him."

"How'd that go?"

Mitch winced as disinfectant hit the raw wound. He let out a slow, hissing breath, then replied, "Let's just say it lacked in warm father-daughter bonding."

"Who won?"

"She hung up on him after announcing that she didn't care if he took away her trust fund, so I'd say it went to the lady."

Hathaway shook his head. "I'm worried about using her. She's a complete amateur."

Mitch looked down at his shoulder as one medic taped a bandage over the gauze and declared him patched up. Mitch reached for his shirt and shrugged it on. Must get a new one before they left. This one was torn and blood-stained. "But that's exactly the point. You take one look at her and see a spoiled little rich girl who couldn't possibly be involved in any kind of covert ops. She's the perfect cover."

"It's not her ability to act as a cover I'm worried about. What if something goes wrong? She doesn't have the slightest idea how to handle herself in a tight spot."

"She did pretty damned good yesterday with bullets flying all over the place and dogfighting a cigarette boat at seventy miles per hour—like a pro by the way. Kept her wits about her. She was a big help to me."

Hathaway didn't answer right away. He picked on some non-existent lint on his slacks. Looked like he was stalling. "Our background check on her shows she's a hell of a sailor. Been around boats her whole life. She and her brother won some New England championship a while back sailing Hobie Cats."

"So my catamaran idea is a go, then?" Mitch asked eagerly. Why was he so damned desperate to spend more time with Kinsey? She was bound to end up being a royal pain in the ass.

Hathaway sighed heavily. "Yeah. It's a go. But if she hurts a single hair on her pretty little head, you can expect to answer directly to daddy dearest. Is that understood?"

Mitch nodded. A little voice at the back of his head hollered. *What was he getting himself into?*

Hathaway added direly, "I'm not kidding. Congressman Hollingsworth will have your head on a platter."

"I hear ya, Commander. Loud and clear."

Another sigh out of Hathaway. Poor guy wasn't

happy about this development in the least. "All right, then. You've got your girl."

Mitch shot him a startled look. His girl? Yikes.

And yet, it did feel odd to Mitch to be separated from Kinsey for even this long. They'd been together less than a day, and he already felt some sort of link to her. Not good. Not good at all. He sat through his final briefing—no significant political developments to report in Cuba in the past couple of days. His mission was cleared to proceed.

Hathaway leaned against the wall. "If you're sure about this, go collect the lady and be on your way."

Mitch scowled. "I'm not sure about anything."

Hathaway shrugged. "Should be an interesting mission, at any rate."

Great. Just what he wanted. An *interesting* mission. He stepped out into a hallway that, like all the others in this facility was low and rough, hewn directly out of the volcanic bedrock. Jennifer would no doubt take Kinsey to her office to finish prepping her for the mission. He strode down the long hallways toward Kinsey, all but running to her. The fastest way from the military side of the facility to the civilian area was back through the main ops center, so he cut across there, even though the staff didn't like through traffic. The floor supervisor threw him a dirty look before it occurred to Mitch what he was doing. He was not some lovesick kid who needed to chase around after Kinsey like an eager puppy, dammit. He screeched to a halt, glancing around more than a little abashed.

A red flash lit up the twenty-foot-tall global map on the far wall. A second look showed it to be in the Middle East.

Most of the floor staff typed busily on their computers for a few moments. "Problem?" he asked one of them.

"Nah. Just a mundane explosion. Looks like a car bomb from the heat signature and seismic readings."

While Mitch had the guy's attention, he asked, "What's that yellow flashing light in the Bahamas?"

"Emergency locator transmitter. Probably a civilian boat in distress. They use equipment similar to the panic button you're equipped with. Whenever an ELT goes off, it shows up red on our screen. Once we've identified it and eliminated the signal as something we need to respond to, it's changed to yellow on the big board."

"Here's hoping I'm never a dot on your screen."

"Oh, you are. When you go into Cuba, you'll go up there as a green dot. We'll track your position in dicator 24/7."

"You mean the one in my arm?"

"Yeah."

He'd always wondered who the little gizmo they'd surgically implanted under his biceps a few years back talked to. Now he knew. He was a green dot on somebody's radar. He continued across the floor and up the stairs to Agent-in-Charge Blackfoot's office, bounding up them three at a time. His stomach jumping, he knocked on the closed door.

"Come in," Jennifer's husky voice called.

He stepped in. Jennifer wore her issue jeans and T-shirt, Native American jewelry, her long hair glossy and black. He glanced around. No sign of Kinsey. Quick alarm flared in his gut. Jennifer was sitting on her sofa with another woman, a striking brunette. Maybe a subject matter expert here to brief Kinsey. Except…her mouth was vaguely familiar…his brain locked up. No way.

He stared closely at the brunette. "Kinsey?" he asked incredulously.

She laughed gaily, her distinctive dimples flashing. Yup, that was Kinsey. He burst out, "What have you done to your hair?"

Jennifer replied. "We had to make sure she isn't recognized by paparazzi and pesky celebrity seekers when she takes you to Cuba, and you have to admit, she looks a great deal different as a brunette."

He examined her more closely. Her gentleness and unique spark still shone out of her eyes, and the refined bones and perfect smile were the same. Maybe at a glance she looked different, but when he looked closely, it was definitely her. He was still going to have to beat men off with sticks whenever she was around.

"Like my disguise?" Kinsey asked.

"You'll do," he said gruffly.

The two women exchanged smiling glances. Now what was that all about?

Jennifer murmured, "See what I mean?"

Kinsey nodded. "Yup. Uncomfortable. I'll keep it in mind."

"Are you two accusing me of being uncomfortable around women?"

Kinsey looked him square in the eye and said blandly, "If the shoe fits."

"I do fine around women. I just don't like working with them."

"Oh really?" Jennifer replied, a distinct edge in her voice.

He glared over at her. "You know perfectly well I don't have a problem with you. I meant in the field."

"You've never worked with a female operative before, so how can you be so sure you won't like it?"

"Operative being the key word," he shot back. "Kinsey's an amateur. She has no business playing spy. I'm happy to use her to get into Cuba, but she's not staying with me a minute longer than it takes me to track down Camarillo and kill him."

The laughter sparkling in Kinsey's eyes blinked out, leaving behind only hurt. Damn, he was a heel. He mentally kicked himself.

"Okay you two. Off you go," Jennifer said, standing up. "You've got a helicopter scheduled in a little under an hour, and by the time you collect the gear we've assembled for you, change into deck clothes, and ride back to the surface, you'll have to hustle to make it." She glared over at him. "And you behave yourself. Be nice."

He'd have protested that his manners were just fine, but Kinsey stood up just then and Mitch gulped. She was wearing a thin wraparound dress made of a muted floral fabric, typical of what Cuban women might wear. It clung to her body in all the right places and plunged just enough between her breasts to make a guy's eyes want to dip downward constantly. He preferred the sloppy T-shirt and bikini to this. This made her look intensely feminine. Kissable. Like she needed to be swept up in his arms and danced with.

He didn't dance with his partner, dammit!

He led the way in silence back to the submarine loading dock. It was beneath him to sulk, but he couldn't help himself. Kinsey put a hand on his arm to steady herself as she climbed into the minisub, and his heart rate must've jumped twenty points. He had to pull himself together, and fast, if this mission wasn't going to fail colossally.

He faked sleeping for most of the ride to the surface. It was Kinsey who actually leaned forward to touch his knee, causing his eyes to fly open in alarm.

"I think it's time to put the blindfold back on."

He glanced outside. Dim turquoise light filtered down through the water outside, casting a flickering glow across the interior of the submarine. She was right. They were nearing the surface. He slipped the blindfold over her eyes, jerking his hands away clumsily when his fingertips brushed against the back of her neck. He was going to have to get over this phobia of touching her so they could—he broke off the thought sharply. No touching on this mission. Definitely no touching.

It wasn't five minutes later when the hatch opened, he climbed out, and turned around to see Kinsey's hand held up to him for balance as she climbed out of the sub. So much for his no touching rule. Her soft hand rested easily in his as she smiled her thanks up in his general direction. A growl of frustration built in the back of his throat. Exasperated, he tucked her hand under his elbow, closing his eyes in silent desperation as she leaned in against him for security. He couldn't blame her. He'd hate being deprived of his sight like this.

"Where to now?" she murmured.

"Your chariot awaits you," he grumbled.

"You mean the helicopter?"

"Yup." He led her carefully under the spinning rotors

and guided her into the chopper. In no time they were skimming across the ocean, open water stretching away on all sides of them. He leaned forward and unmasked her. She blinked, squinting against the light and smiled over at him.

"All this secrecy and mystery is fun."

"Fun? Are you kidding? This is a serious mission. Jennifer did brief you on what we're supposed to be doing, didn't she?"

"Yes. We're going to Cuba to gather intelligence on a possible plot to assassinate a high-ranking Cuban official who is…friendly…toward the United States."

"No, I am going to Cuba to do that. *We* are going to Cuba so *I* can find and kill Camarillo, and then *you* are going home."

The official who was the target of his mission, a man named Alejandro Zaragosa, had been passing information to the United States for nigh unto thirty years. He was an extremely valuable asset in need of protection. But in all honesty, Mitch was much more intent on finding and killing Camarillo. Kinsey wouldn't be safe until the guy was dead.

She shrugged, still far too animated for her own good. He growled, "Where in that equation do you come up with any fun whatsoever?"

"It's a beautiful day. The sun is shining, the sky is blue, and we're setting off on a grand adventure. What more could you ask for?"

He scowled. "This isn't a game, dammit."

"Oh, lighten up," she teased gently. "Don't take yourself so seriously."

A babe in the woods. She had *no* idea what they

were headed into. His scowl deepened. He retreated into stony silence, crossing his arms over his chest. She did the same. He could swear she was mimicking him just to get his goat. Well, it wasn't going to work. He uncrossed his arms and shifted uncomfortably in his seat.

The fast chopper skimmed over the ocean for several exceedingly long hours. Mitch was abjectly grateful when the crew chief finally opened the back hatch and swung a pulley mechanism out the door.

"What's he doing?" Kinsey shouted over the noise.

"Rigging up the winch," he shouted back. "You and I will jump out of the 'copter, but the other captain will have to get hauled up into this bird."

"What are you talking about?"

"Didn't Jennifer tell you we were coming out here to pick up a boat?"

"She said we'd be dropped off at a catamaran, but she didn't say anything about jumping out of a helicopter into the Caribbean."

He rolled his eyes. "What did you think getting dropped off meant?"

"Certainly not that!"

He grinned. "Welcome to my world, princess."

He tried not to watch as she stripped off her dress and stuffed it into the waterproof duffel bag Jennifer had given her to hold all her stuff. The sight of Kinsey in a bikini ripped all the air out of his chest. Damn, that woman had curves in all the right places. His gut flared with desire, bright and hot. She was interested in him. If he played his cards right—

No card playing on this mission. None of that at all!

A movement out of the corner of his eye caused his head to snap around. The crew chief was taking a long, appreciative look at Kinsey. Mitch surged up out of his seat and all but shoved the guy out of the helicopter. He managed to control himself in time to merely place himself between Kinsey and the guy's line of sight, but a need to do violence made his palms itch.

The look of apprehension on Kinsey's face as she stepped into the doorway of the chopper and looked down reminded him of just how risky a job he had. But, to her credit, she climbed out onto the tread and gamely jumped off. He didn't think she had it in her. The seas were calm and the pilot was good, so the bird was no more than twelve feet or so above the water. Still, to an amateur, it must've looked like they were a mile up. He stepped off the skid and endured the cold shock of slamming into the water. His eyes tightly closed, he made his way up to the surface and swam easily over to the catamaran. Kinsey was already aboard, shaking saltwater out of her eyes and having a look at the vessel's equipment.

While the outgoing captain briefed her up, Mitch hauled in their waterproof bags of equipment, both of which had been tethered to his waist and tossed out of the 'copter with him. In a few minutes, the captain bade them farewell and jumped overboard, swimming over to the padded loop that would lift him into the chopper. Mitch watched the crew chief efficiently haul up the guy. The chopper peeled away sharply and sped off into the distance.

And then they were alone. Relief at having her to himself once more filled him. Silence descended around them.

"Now what, Tonto?" Kinsey asked.

"Head for Cuba, Kemosabe."

"It's about fifty miles due north of us."

"How soon can we be there?"

She turned her face into the breeze. "If these winds hold up, sometime this evening."

"Let's do it."

She nodded and moved fore to weigh anchor and hoist the main sail. He pitched in to help haul on the various lines she pointed out, and before long, they were skimming across the water at a decent clip. He stepped inside the low, flat cabin slung between the vessel's twin hulls. It was compact and he more or less had to crawl around on his knees inside, but it was well fitted out.

"Nice boat," Kinsey commented from behind him.

"Aren't you supposed to be on deck doing the captain thing?"

"The sails are trimmed, the wind is steady, and the autopilot's got the helm. I can spare a couple minutes to have a look around. Where did your people scare up this vessel on such short notice?"

"I have no idea. Maybe someone called in a favor, maybe a little cash got spread around. But that's how the H.O.T. Watch staff works. If an operator needs something, it's taken care of. That big room full of folks sitting at phones and computers is jammed with miracle workers."

Her hand strayed up toward her head. "I was impressed when they came up with hair dye and clothes that fit me on such short notice.

"What does 'hot' in hot watch refer to?"

He grinned. "H-O-T. Hunter Operation Team."

Enlightenment dawned. "And the gang in the volcano watches you. Hence, H.O.T. Watch."

"You got it."

He examined her critically. "You make a good brunette."

A blush stained her cheeks. "Uhh, I'd better go find a cover-up. I don't need the entire Cuban navy ogling me."

No kidding. If one crew chief had driven him nuts, imagine how a whole boatload of sailors would affect him.

Kinsey stared down at the boat's controls, the dials an unfocused blob before her eyes. Every time Mitch turned that golden gaze of his on her, she melted into a puddle of nerves. She had to stop that! This was her chance to do something real, something important, and she wasn't going to blow it because she couldn't corral her runaway lust for a man who barely gave her the time of day.

The sunset tonight was even more spectacular than yesterday's and Mitch came out on deck to watch its magnificent display streak across the sky. He lounged on the broad sun deck, his hands clasped behind his head as he gazed up at the sky. He looked like a panther at rest, all sleek feline grace and explosive power waiting to spring into action.

Intense awareness of being alone with him in the middle of a vast ocean struck her. She'd made a giant leap of trust to place herself at his mercy like this. For she held no illusions about her ability to fend him off if he tried any funny business with her. Her mind wandered idly. What would she do if he made a pass at her? She was half tempted to accept his offer. Okay, more than half tempted. She seriously hoped he gave it a go. Unfortunately, he would never take her seriously if she initiated anything personal between them. But that didn't mean she couldn't wish for him to do it. She sighed. Fat chance of that happening with Mr. Mission-first.

When no more than a red glow remained on the far horizon, he made his way back to the helm. "Mother Nature did good today," he commented.

She glanced askance at the streaks of clouds fading from lavender to dark gray overhead. "Yeah, but those are rolled cirrus clouds. They indicate a front moving in." When he didn't show comprehension of the threat they posed, she elaborated, "And that means rain. Storms. We've got to get off the water and soon. The wind is dying down, so I'm going to start up the engines and motor us in close to the Cuban coast."

He drawled, "How long till we arrive?"

"An hour, maybe a little more." She liked the lazy side of the predator. He was easier to be with when he was relaxed like this, not constantly eyeing everything around him like he expected an attack at any second.

"I'll be back."

He disappeared below while she cranked up the twin diesels. She'd just finished retrimming the rudders when he emerged, carrying his black duffel bag. "Ever shoot a gun?" he bit out.

Drat. *Back in commando mode.* "I've handled a pistol or two, but I'm no great expert."

He stepped up behind her, invading her personal space with his broad shoulders and bristling male energy. His arm came around her right side to lay a big, scary revolver on the instrument panel beside the steering wheel.

"Colt .45," he murmured. "Not a lady's weapon, but it'll stop a Mack Truck."

Involuntarily, she stepped back from the gun…and right into the wall that was Mitch Perovski. His strength and bulk were such that he didn't even budge when she banged into him. She about jumped out of her skin.

"Easy," he murmured. "It won't bite you."

No, but he might. Aggressive male potency engulfed her, and she edged forward to put a few inches between them. It didn't help. "Is it loaded?"

A rusty chuckle tickled her ear. "Wouldn't be good for much if it wasn't. Don't fire it until you're positive you'll hit your target. It only has six shots. Use them wisely."

Had the temperature just dropped ten degrees? She rubbed her arms to chase away the sudden goose bumps. *He was giving an untrained civilian a lethal weapon?* He must be scared spitless of this Camarillo guy to be teaching her to handle a gun like this.

"Pick it up," he murmured.

She lifted the pistol. It was heavy. Cold. Awkward in her hand. She lurched as his arms came around her from behind. His right hand closed over hers, wrapping her fingers more securely around the scored grip.

"Hold it nose high in front of you with your arms straight. Like this."

Damned if his mouth wasn't practically against her ear. Searing heat ripped through her, followed by embarrassment. Shyness. Intensely sexual awareness of him.

His cheek came to rest against her ear, slightly stubbly. Warm. *Intimate.* His arms slid up under hers.

The silky hair on his forearms tickled the undersides of her arms, and his elbows gently squeezed the sides of her breasts. *Whoa, baby.*

"Look down the barrel." Was that amusement or urgency—or something else altogether—pulling his voice tight like that? She couldn't tell. And didn't have the nerve to turn around and look.

"Don't worry about being accurate. At close range, a strike anywhere on the bad guy from a .45 will stop him cold. Rest the bottom of your right fist in the palm of your left hand. Push with the right, pull with the left. It'll steady the gun. Like this. Got it?"

She nodded fractionally. It was all the unbearable tension in her neck would allow for. But wrapped around her like red on a rose, he apparently felt the microscopic movement.

"When you pull the trigger, this sucker will kick up in the air. Hard. Let it. Then, bring it back down into firing position, aim, and fire again."

"How do I aim?" Good grief. Was that *her* voice all husky and breathless like that?

"Look straight down the barrel. Whatever you see directly over the tip of the barrel is roughly what you'll hit. Fire at the bad guy's belly button. The torso is a big target and you're more likely to hit it than if you aim at something small like a head or a knee. Actual aiming of a weapon is more complicated than that, but we don't have time for more details right now. I'll show you the fine points some other time."

"It's a date." She froze. *Had she said that aloud?*

She'd swear his mouth turned up, smiling against the

shell of her ear as he murmured, "Deal." Streaks of pure sex tore through her. Surely he felt her burning alive in his arms.

His lips definitely were moving against her ear now. "Don't fire toward me in a fight and I won't fire toward you. That way we won't hit each other by accident. Got it?"

Her knees all but buckled out from under her. Breathing fast and shallow, she nodded.

"One last thing. If I go down fighting it out with Camarillo and he's about to catch you, do yourself a favor. Save one bullet for yourself. Up into the brain through the back of the mouth is the most effective."

His words shocked her like ice water down her shirt. She pivoted to stare at him. *Big mistake.* She drew up short, chest to chest with him. His arms, still wrapped around her, gathered her close. *Kowabunga.* His eyes, blazing hollows in the shadowed planes of his face, incinerated her.

Was she insane? He'd just suggested the best way to *kill* herself. And she was lusting after him? "Are you serious?" she exclaimed.

He looked her dead in the eye. The last expression she would ever expect to see flashed into his gaze. *Compassion.* And that rattled her to the core.

"Promise me," he said with quiet urgency. "I need to know you won't let Camarillo capture you. I can't afford to make a stupid decision in the middle of a fight because I'm trying to protect the girl."

"The girl can take care of herself," Kinsey retorted dryly. She wriggled to free herself from his suddenly suffocating embrace. His arms fell away immediately and night air replaced them, embracing her in dread's icy clasp.

"Without mincing words, Camarillo is one of the baddest SOB's on the planet. When we engage him, I need you to keep your wits about you. If bullets start flying, get down low, stay out of the line of fire, and don't try to be a hero. I'll do the rest."

"You're sounding suspiciously like a macho jerk."

"I'm a macho *bastard* in a firefight. But I'll be *your* macho bastard. So stay out of my way and do what I tell you. All right?"

She nodded. With every passing second he was becoming more grim. More focused. Wiped clean of emotion. *Ready to kill.*

"How long till the Cuban coast?" he asked shortly.

She glanced at the radar, which was starting to paint the coastline. "At current speed, about twenty minutes."

"Can you limp in from here on sails only?"

She nodded.

"It's time to sabotage the engines, then."

She grabbed a wrench from the toolbox in the cabin and opened up the vessel's pontoon hatches. She went to work on the fuel system for it shared duty with both engines. If she truly wanted to be disabled and need believable emergency repairs, she had to take out both engines with whatever she broke. Her best bet was the fuel pump. If it failed, the fuel lines would lose pressure, air would enter the lines, and both engines' fuel systems would have to be purged of air all the way down to the fuel injectors. Not an easy thing to do at sea. Particularly for a lone, hand-wringing female at sea with no clue how to do the job.

In point of fact, she'd seen the job done a couple of

times and, in a real emergency, could probably muddle her way through it. But what the Cubans didn't know wouldn't hurt them. The boat would need to be towed into port, a new fuel pump ordered and installed, and both her fuel systems purged. All in all, it should take upward of a week.

She gave the fuel pump one last whack with her wrench for good measure. The engines made awful sucking sounds for a few moments, then sputtered and cut out. Silence. No more diesel power for them from here on out. She inched forward inside the pontoon to the escape hatch. The space in here was cramped and claustrophobic, but it certainly was big enough to conceal a man and all his gear.

They were ready. Now all she had to do was make her way into port. And pray. Pray they were allowed into Cuba, and that Mitch was better than Camarillo. Menace drew near. Its cool touch slid up her spine like a psychopathic lover. And they waited. She stood behind the wheel, terrified, minding the boat by rote, while Mitch crouched at the forward limit of the deck, peering at the sea through big, 30x binoculars.

For an about-to-be hunted man, he looked a lot like a predator in wait. Abject terror was going to shatter her into a million pieces any second, but he looked as steady as a rock. *Show-off.*

"Time to contact?" Mitch called.

She glanced down at the radar screen. "Fifteen minutes at this forward speed until we hit Cuban territorial waters. Their Coast Guard should come out to have a look at us pretty quickly after that."

Mitch nodded and made his way back to the pilot house. "Ready?" he murmured.

She looked into his eyes. And then it hit. Panic. Paralyzing, brain-numbing, panic.

Mitch swore under his breath. "There's nothing to worry about. Just be yourself. You're Kinsey Hollingsworth. Your boat has lost a couple vital systems—which it in fact, has. You need repairs, which is the God's honest truth. You don't have to be clever or lie or try to keep your cool. Be upset. Be panicked. Be worried about being arrested for having to land in Cuba."

She nodded. That was exactly what Jennifer Blackfoot had told her to do. So why did she feel like she was going to throw up any second?

Mitch stepped forward with that preternaturally quick grace of his, his powerful arms sweeping her up against him in an enveloping hug. He murmured into her hair, "Hey. I know you can do this."

"Yeah. Assuming I can keep my lunch down."

"Ahh. Pre-mission jitters. I get them all the time."

"Do you have them now?"

"No, I got mine on the chopper ride out here."

She mumbled into his chest, "Liar. You've got nerves of steel."

A low rumble of laughter shook his chest.

She lifted her head to glare up at him. Their gazes locked. Their wills tangled for a moment, hers skeptical, his certain. And the banked fire in the back of his eyes began to build, heating until it glowed like a lava flow, incinerating everything in its path. She stared into the mesmerizing depths of his gaze, fascinated, inevitably drawn into him.

His index finger touched her chin. Tipped her face up. And slowly, slowly, like a panther stalking its prey, he closed in on her. Except unlike the unwary antelope, she saw him coming. And merely watched and waited. For a moment, she contemplated fleeing for her life, but discarded the idea as ridiculous. In the last moment before their lips touched, when her common sense shouted its indignation at her foolishness, she realized she'd been waiting for this ever since the first moment she'd laid eyes on him. With a sigh of relief, she surrendered to the kiss.

His mouth was warm and firm against hers, exploring hers gently. And then, without warning, he groaned in the back of his throat and his arms swept her up against him, lifting her completely off the ground. Crushed in his embrace, she strained even closer, desperate for more of him.

"We shouldn't..." he mumbled against her mouth just before he devoured her whole, with tongue and lips and body.

"But I want it. I want you...." she mumbled back just before she returned the favor.

He cursed under his breath as he let her feet slide to the ground. Crying out in dismay, she flung her arms around his neck. He stumbled for a moment, then planted his powerful legs, absorbed her weight, and plunged his hands into her hair, dragging her mouth up to his for more. He kissed her desperately, aggressively, like a starving man.

"This is madness," he bit out.

"Glorious madness," she agreed, dragging his head down to her.

Another groan, wrung from deep within him made her heart leap with triumph. "If we don't stop now, I'm going to tear your clothes off, take you inside, and make love to you until neither of us can walk."

She took a step toward the cabin, pulling him with her. He laughed, gathering her close. "We'll be in Cuban territorial waters in a few minutes, and their navy should arrive about two minutes after that. I've got to crawl into my coffin or else they'll see me."

The words only partially penetrated the haze of unadulterated desire roaring through her brain. The taste of him, smoky and dark, swirled through her head until she could hardly think about anything else.

Gently, he peeled her arms from around his neck. She followed him to the starboard pontoon hatch and handed his duffel bag in after him. The thing was shockingly heavy. Must be chock-full of more giant guns like the one he'd shown her earlier.

As he stretched out on his back and nodded up at her, she couldn't resist. She leaned down into the opening and kissed him one last time. "Mmm. You taste amazing." She sighed.

"Close the hatch," he said grimly. Then he added, "But hold that thought."

Smiling dreamily, she brought the fiberglass down into place, locking the latch that held it in place. She made her way back to the pilot house and absently checked their heading. If she stayed on this source, she'd run smack dab into the south coast of Cuba. She ought to be rehearsing a speech for the Cuban navy, but the only thought that kept running through her mind over and over was, *that man could really, really kiss.*

She wanted more of that. Lots more.

She became aware of a faint sound carrying across

the water from the north…the mechanical rumble of a boat motor incoming. Undoubtedly the Cuban navy.

Showtime.

Chapter 6

A male voice shouted through a bullhorn at her in heavily accented English, "You have entered Cuban territorial waters. Turn around and leave or prepare to be boarded!"

Kinsey squinted into the blinding glare of the floodlight they pointed at her. She called back, "My engines have conked out. I'm adrift. Can you tow me to someplace where I can make repairs?"

She thought she made out scowls behind the floodlight, but it was hard to see. The man shouted back, "How many souls on board?"

"Just me."

"Are you declaring a maritime emergency?"

Ahh. The officialese so they could legally tow her ashore. "Yes, I am."

After a long pause, the voice called back, "We will send a man over to secure a tow line."

What? Like she couldn't tie a proper tow line herself? She didn't argue, however. If they thought she was actually helpless, all the better. The catamaran rocked as the Cuban vessel pulled up alongside. A sailor leaped across the gap between the boats, hauling with him the end of a heavy line. He didn't tie the rope to the optimal tow point, but the one he chose wouldn't capsize her, so she let it go. The Cuban sailor manned her steering wheel in silence for the slow ride to port, while she stretched out and made herself comfortable on the sun deck. The Cuban navy crew made no secret of enjoying the view of her, lounging in her skimpy bikini and sloppy T-shirt. *Look all you want, boys.* The more distracted they were, the less likely they were to think about searching her vessel for contraband.

They pulled into port in Cienfuegos, a decent-size city on the south coast of Cuba. The navy cutter hauled her directly to a marina catering to pleasure craft. One of their men went ashore, and in a few minutes, they maneuvered her into a slip near the end of a long, wooden dock that had seen better days.

What looked like a Customs official and maybe a policeman accompanied the navy man back to her boat. No surprise, the Customs guy wanted her passport. He disappeared back down the dock with it, mumbling about needing to work up an emergency visa for her. It made her nervous to see that vitally important document being carried off like that, but she wasn't in any position to protest.

The policeman announced, "I will need to search your boat. Any unauthorized vessel which comes ashore is required to be searched."

What else could she do? She shrugged and nodded her understanding, her mind racing. She had to stop him! But how? Anything she did to make the guy suspicious would make him doubly intent upon combing through the boat. Thankfully, he started in the cabin, which gave her a few minutes to think.

When he stepped outside once more, she stepped into his path, subtly herding him away from the foredeck and the hatches to the pontoons. "Here. Let me unlock the map cabinets for you. They're back here, at the pilot station."

She led the policeman to the rear of the vessel. As she'd hoped, he continued his exterior search of the boat from the aft end and working his way forward. She even let him open the fore, port pontoon hatch before she pulled out her cell phone.

"Do you mind if I make a phone call?" she asked politely.

"Who do you wish to call?"

"My father. He works in Washington, D.C."

The reference to Washington brought a faintly surprised look to the cop's face.

She continued chattily, "I think I can get cell phone coverage here. And Daddy has a satellite phone. He has to, so when a bill comes up in Congress, he can be notified to go vote."

That shot the policeman's eyebrows straight up. In fact, it caused him to step away from her—toward the dock—and pull out his own cell phone. He held a quick, muttered conversation in Spanish. She edged closer to him twice, and both times, he moved away from her, closer to shore. The third time she edged closer as if to listen in, he actually stepped up onto the dock. Perfect.

The Customs man came into sight, carrying some paperwork. The policeman finished his call, and Kinsey cheerfully pocketed her cell phone. "Not working. Looks like I'll have to wait until I can get access to a landline. Any chance I can get a hotel room or something so I can clean up and make that call? Daddy will be terribly worried until I report in. Goodness knows who he'll send after me if I don't contact him soon."

The policeman answered nervously, "Uhh, certainly we can arrange a room for you, Señorita Hollingsworth."

"Thank you so much!" she gushed. "I could just hug you."

The guy seemed flustered at the prospect. He was saved from having to reply by the Customs official handing her back her passport. "The light-blue paper inside is your temporary visa. It is good for two weeks. I assume your boat can be repaired and you can be on your way in that amount of time?"

She batted her eyes at him helplessly. "Well, I don't know. I'll need a mechanic to have a look at things and make an estimate. But I hope I can be out of your hair in a few days. You are all being so kind to me. I really appreciate this. I was starting to get worried out there. I only had food and water for a day or so more. It never occurred to me that I might need extra supplies. I was only going out for a short sail."

Both men threw her looks that damned her ignorance of basic boating safety, and she took the looks of rebuke without protest. "I know. I know. Boating 101. I should've thrown a few emergency supplies onboard just in case. I will from now on, I swear."

She put a hand on the policeman's arm. "Now, about that shower. What do I have to do to sweet talk you into leading me to some hot water and soap?"

Both men reached out to help her ashore, and with a smile of apology at the Customs man, she took the policeman's hand. "Is there someplace nearby so I can keep an eye on my boat and monitor the repairs?"

"There is a nice place just up the beach. It's called La Bonita. I will help you check in and get settled if you wish."

She let them lead her up the dock and away from the catamaran…and Mitch. Mission accomplished. She'd distracted the cop before he could finish his search. If she wasn't mistaken, Mitch owed her one.

She wasn't clear on how Mitch was supposed to sneak ashore and hook up with her again. He'd told her they'd have to wing it once they got to Cuba.

La Bonita was an old building, shabby, but in reasonable repair. And it had a lingering attractiveness. Like a Hollywood glamour queen who'd seen her prime thirty or forty years ago. The policeman was helpful—too helpful—in getting her settled into a "nice" room. She began to wonder if it was bugged or something, the way he insisted on getting a specific room on a high floor with a view of the water, ostensibly so she could keep an eye on her boat.

Finally, the guy left. In case the place was bugged, she did exactly what they would expect of her. She didn't actually want to talk to her father, so she called his office and left a message on his answering machine. Plus, the machine made it clear that she was, indeed, calling Congressman Hollingsworth.

Next, she jumped into the shower. The pressure of the water wasn't great and it smelled like sulphur, but it was hot and removed the feeling of salt crusted on her skin. Did she dare go back to the boat tonight to try to free Mitch? He'd said for her to sit tight, and knowing him, he'd get mad if she disobeyed his instructions. He struck her as that sort of guy.

She flipped through the television channels. Her Spanish wasn't up to the rapid-fire dialect of the programming, so she turned out the lights and went to bed. It took awhile for her fraying nerves to settle down, but she eventually drifted off.

How long she was asleep, she had no idea. But one moment, she was peacefully resting, and the next, a powerful hand was pressed over her mouth. She all but jumped out of her skin as something heavy rolled on top of her, pressing her down into the mattress and immobilizing her.

"It's me," a voice breathed in her ear. *Mitch.* Warm relief flooded her. She relaxed, releasing the panic clenching her muscles. And then the sensation of lying beneath Mitch in a blatantly suggestive pose exploded in her brain. His knee pressed between her thighs, supporting his weight, but also pinning her so she couldn't possibly move out from under him. His eyes closed briefly. When they opened, the blazing sexual awareness in them all but lit the entire room.

"Don't say anything," he gritted out under his breath. "The room may be bugged. Understood?"

She nodded, and his hand lifted away from her mouth. He pressed up and away from her with swift power, and her body ached with sudden loss.

She watched in silence as his dark silhouette prowled around her room, searching with ruthless efficiency. He stopped three times and pointed—once at a lamp, once at the clock-radio, and once at a hinge in the bathroom door. Great. So the two of them knew where the bugs were. Now what?

He came over to the bed and lifted the covers. She was on the verge of getting up when he crawled in beside her. Stunned, she scooted over to make room for him in the narrow double bed. His muscular bulk took up most of it, at least until he turned on his side and gathered her close against him. Yowza. She liked this even better than before. She couldn't help it. She snuggled up against him—in the name of giving him enough room, of course.

It was like cuddling up to a brick. Albeit a warm, vital, sexy one. He pulled the covers over their heads and pressed his mouth to her ear. "Three bugs. Audio only. You need to get dressed and pack your stuff without making any noise. Can you do that?"

She nodded, and his lips accidentally brushed against her neck. She all but groaned at the sensation. His arm tightened around her momentarily, but then he was gone, rolling away silently and disappearing into the shadows by the door. Her pulse raced, and parts of her throbbed that seriously didn't need to be doing any throbbing just now. Lord, that man was magnetic!

She tiptoed to her bag of gear and eased out a pair of black slacks and a dark shirt to match Mitch's dark clothing. She didn't want to risk closing the bathroom door, so she stepped into the shower to change and prayed Mitch didn't do a drive by in here to see how she was coming. Although the prospect of him seeing her undressed made that whole throbbing thing start back up again.

She tiptoed back out into the room and carefully repacked her overnight bag. Fortunately she hadn't gotten much out of it earlier. Mitch picked it up and gestured for her to follow him. He opened the hallway door a crack and peered outside cautiously. He slipped outside quickly and she followed him as he raced down the hallway on the balls of his feet, swift and silent. Man, she'd hate to be on the receiving end of this guy's predatory stealth.

Down a concrete-and-steel stairwell, and out onto a loading dock, she did her best not to make too much of a racket behind him. Still not talking, he waved her into an alley, which he sprinted down. He turned into a side street and darted across it, then down another alley with her in tow. Good thing she hit the treadmill on a regular basis. He was moving fast and showing no signs of slowing down.

And then all of a sudden, he pulled up beside a vintage car that made her stare. It was big and black and sleek, all chrome and fenders and tiny windows. It looked like a gangster car out of the 1930s. She ventured to whisper, "What's this?"

"Our ride. Like it?" he murmured as he opened the driver side door and tossed her bag into the backseat. "Slide in. I'll drive," he directed under his breath.

The seat was cracked vinyl that scratched the back of her legs. The dials and needles looked original to the vehicle, yellowed with age and from another era.

Mitch closed the door and started the car. He pulled away from the curb.

"Where did you get this thing?"

"I bought it. Like it?"

"You bought it? How did you have time to get ashore and buy a car already?"

He laughed. "I was off the boat before you stepped off the dock. Nice misdirect of that cop, by the way. I didn't know you had it in you."

"What would you have done if I hadn't distracted him?"

"I'd scooted all the way to the back end of the pontoon and was behind the engine. He'd never have seen me unless he crawled into the pontoon, in which case…"

"In which case, what?"

Mitch sighed. "In which case, I'd have neutralized him and you'd have had to make some excuse to the Customs guy about where his cop friend disappeared to."

This man was a killer. Her mind knew the thought to be true, but her heart rejected the thought. She was attracted to him, darn it. Yet there was no denying what and who he was. Heck, she'd seen him kill with her own eyes. Although given that he had saved both her life and his, any murderous overtones were wiped away by the necessary self-defense of the act.

Her half of the deal was complete. She'd snuck Mitch into Cuba. Now all he had to do was uphold his end of the deal and eliminate Camarillo as a threat to her. Then they'd be even. She would walk away. And then she'd face the unenviable task of figuring out how to get over wanting to leap on him and kiss him senseless.

* * *

Mitch drove for nearly an hour. Long enough to be well away from Cienfuegos.

"Where are we going?" Kinsey asked from the passenger seat.

"Nowhere in particular at the moment. Just putting distance between you and any authorities who know you're on the island."

"What about your meeting with Zaragosa? Isn't it back in Cienfuegos?"

He shrugged. "It won't happen for another day or two. In the meantime, I'm going to work on tracking down Camarillo." The sooner he got Kinsey out of there, the better it would be for her. An unfamiliar twinge in his gut startled him, and he frowned. What was that about? Was he actually going to miss her when she left? The pampered princess? Nah. No way.

At 3:00 a.m. according to his watch, he turned into a closed gas station and pulled around back beside several other vintage cars waiting for service. He turned off the engine and the lights. In the sudden dark, he pulled out his cell phone and called the Bat Cave. Jennifer Blackfoot picked up. What was *she* doing manning the phones at this hour? She had enough seniority that she didn't have to pull shifts as the night supervisor.

"What are you doing up so late, boss?"

"Problem with another team," she replied shortly. "What's up?"

She clearly had no time to chat, so he got straight to the point. "As my little green dot on the big screen no doubt shows, I'm ashore and with Kinsey. We've got a

car and are about a hundred kilometers from Cienfuegos. What have you got for me on when and where I'm
hooking up with Zaragosa?"

"He says he can't do it. He's being watched too
closely. Says for you to proceed to Havana on your own."

Mitch frowned, his mind racing. Why was the prin-
cipal backing out of helping him? Was Zaragosa setting
him up? Or was it exactly as the man said, a simple
matter of it being too risky for them to make contact?
He growled into the phone, "If I don't have identity
papers, it fundamentally changes the nature of this op.
I'll have to go underground and stay there."

"If the guy won't play ball, there's nothing we can
do about it at this late date. If you were still here we
could work up some fake credentials for you. But as it
is, you're on your own."

"That's the problem," he retorted grimly. "I'm not
on my own."

"Did the Cubans give Kinsey a visa?" Jennifer asked.

"Yeah. Two weeks. She's covered. I'm the only
illegal alien in this outfit."

"Well then, Lancer, I guess you'd better not get caught."

"Hah. I never get caught."

"Let's keep it that way," his boss snapped back.

"Yes, ma'am," he laughed at her.

He disconnected. Kinsey was looking over at him expectantly. "Change of plans. We're not going to meet
Zaragosa after all."

"What does that mean?"

"Not much. We press on as briefed."

"Where's Camarillo?"

"No clue. I thought we'd head for Havana and poke

around a bit. If we hit the right nerve, he may show himself."

"Do you really think it'll be that easy?"

He snorted. "Not a chance. But sometimes you get lucky." He'd left out the part where Camarillo would come after them and try to kill them as soon as he got wind of them. But Kinsey didn't need to know that.

They drove across the island to the north shore, a short journey as the crow flew, but it took several hours. They wound along country roads through farming communities, up into the central highlands, and back down the north slopes toward the Atlantic shore of Cuba. Stands of tropical jungle interspersed with fields in full summer growth, and the overall impression was of a lush, green country. By afternoon, it would be steamy and clothes would cling to damp flesh while beads of sweat rolled down foreheads and necks—and the valley between Kinsey's breasts, his errant imagination had to pipe up and add. Oh, yes. A sexy country, Cuba.

They came into the outskirts of Havana, a sprawling metropolis of several million people. The transition was abrupt. One moment they were cruising through rural acres, and the next, a high-rise city towered around them. Although aged and crumbling around the edges in this particular area, it was a vibrant place, full of noise and bright colors and bustling people.

All well and good, but this was not the side of Havana in which they would find their quarry. They needed the secret side of the city. The night side. The dark side. To that end, he found them a hotel room near the long strip of nightclubs along the shore, left over from the pre-Castro era. Using Kinsey's visa, they checked in.

The room looked like it hadn't been redecorated since Castro came to power in 1959, but it was clean. And dark. Like any good casino hotel room, it was set up for the occupant to sleep all day in anticipation of gambling all night. Thick, lined, velvet curtains blocked out the bright, Caribbean sunlight.

"You'd do well to take a nap, Kinsey. We'll be out late tonight."

"Doing what?" she asked curiously.

He grinned. "Partying the night away."

She frowned. "To what end?"

"We're going hunting. We're going to catch ourselves a killer."

Chapter 7

Kinsey frowned at the dress Mitch handed to her. Jennifer Blackfoot had predicted this would be the first dress he would want her to wear when the woman had pulled it off a rack of assorted clothing in the H.O.T. Watch complex. It had looked okay on a hanger, but right now it looked like hardly more than a dish towel. And it was red.

She shimmied into the slinky little sheath in the bathroom and looked at herself critically. It wasn't something she'd normally dream of choosing for herself, but she had to admit, she didn't look half bad in it. The red complemented her newly dark hair, and the short hemline made her legs look a mile long. She plucked a scarlet silk hibiscus out of the flower arrangement on the bathroom counter and tucked it behind her left ear. A dab of perfume and she was ready to go hunting. As it were. She couldn't fathom what sort of hunting Mitch had in mind with her dressed like this.

She stepped out of the bathroom. Mitch glanced up from the gun he was cleaning. Froze. Looked all the way down to her toes and back up again to her eyes. Unaccountably, she was nervous. Usually, she didn't give a flip what other people thought of her looks, but she wanted to meet with Mitch's approval. Silence stretched out between them as he devoured the sight of her.

She finally said, "If you only tell me 'that'll do,' I'm putting my sloppy T-shirt over this thing before we go out."

He moved so fast she hardly had time to jump. But all of a sudden he loomed before her, his expression blacker than the night and more dangerous than sin. His hands were on her, cupping her derriere, climbing up her back, drawing her against him, then sliding up one vertebra at a time to the nape of her neck.

His gaze dropped to her mouth, then lifted back to her eyes. He murmured, his voice a low, tight rumble, "I'm going to spend the entire evening imagining ripping that dress off you, throwing you down, and making love to you until you scream."

And now she was going to spend all evening imagining the very same thing.

She swayed, overcome by the images flashing through her head, igniting her body until it was hotter than her dress. "I can't believe what you do to me—" she murmured.

And then his mouth was on hers, his body hard and ready against her, vibrating with desire that set her on fire. Sex had always been a rather intellectual thing for her. You meet an intelligent, fascinating man, get to know him, become friends, contemplate enriching the relationship into something more intimate. And then, you allow attraction to build.

But this…

…This was primal. Completely unthinking lust. It ripped away all veneer of civilized thought from her mind and left her wanting pure, raw sex. Muscle and bone pounding against her and into her, naked flesh on sweaty, naked flesh. Tongues and tangled legs and rasping breath. She wanted *him.*

"Mother of—" he groaned into her mouth. "Kinsey, you're killing me."

"I'm the one losing my mind here."

He pressed his forehead against hers and laughed painfully. "No, no. I'm the one going insane."

"Mmm. Kiss me again, you madman." She reached up, grabbed his head and tugged his mouth down to her. "I can't get enough of you."

"Don't say that to me," he growled harshly. "I'm having a hard enough time not picking you up and carrying you over to that bed as we speak."

"Do it," she whispered. "Whisk me off my feet and make love to me."

A fine shudder passed through him. She felt it from his mouth to his knees against her body. He swore under his breath. "You're officially killing me. We can't do this. Not now."

Piercing loss stabbed her. "Later?" she asked between featherlight kisses.

He lifted his head away to look down at her. She'd never seen him more grim. "I'm not good one-night stand material," he warned. "Once I get in your head,

I'm not going to leave it. When I take you, I'll take all of you."

Was that a promise or a threat? He said it like it was meant to be both. A chill of apprehension chattered through her. She didn't understand exactly what he was telling her, but she knew she ought to pay attention to it and heed the warning. Except the desire pounding through her from head to foot refused to give her any respite to think. Warning or no, she *wanted* him.

Regretfully, he stepped back from her, holding her at arm's length when she would have followed him. "I'm afraid you're going to have to fix your lipstick."

She grinned up at him impishly. "But it looks smashing on you."

He reached up to wipe his mouth, grinning in chagrin while she ducked back into the bathroom to right her hair and makeup. When she emerged, he stood on the far side of the room, over by the door, a study in black. Black slacks, black turtleneck, black hair, black expression. Afraid he couldn't keep his hands off her, huh? She smiled to herself. She could live with that.

They drove in silence, not toward the strip of casinos, but rather toward the center of Havana. They parked on a deserted street in a business district and Mitch held her door for her as she swung her bare legs out of the car and stood up. She caught the sizzling flash in his eyes as he held a hand out for her. Sheesh. Just touching his hand was sending up her temperature alarmingly.

Offering her his elbow, he turned and started down the uneven sidewalk. Her high heels clicked, but his steps made no sound at all.

"Where are we going?" she asked.

"A social club."

"What sort of club is that?"

"Think part restaurant, part nightclub, part disco. They don't officially exist, but everyone who's anyone is a member at one or more of these places."

"If they're members only places, how are we going to get in?"

He grinned over at her. "I belong to several of the best ones."

She started. "How in the heck did you pull that off?"

"This isn't the first time I've been to Cuba. That's why the boys and girls in the bunker sent me to do this job."

"And which job are we working on this evening?"

His visage abruptly went grim in the shadows. "Both of them. But I *want* Camarillo."

"What's the plan?"

He shrugged. "Your job is to distract anyone who asks us too many questions. We'll eat a bit, drink a bit, dance a bit. Circulate."

"So we're going to work the room. What do I do if I spot Camarillo?"

"If he's actually in one of these clubs, duck. He'll start shooting the moment he lays eyes on us."

Shocked, she replied, "Won't he get arrested and go to jail if he shoots someone in downtown Havana?"

"Not him. As a boy, he fought beside Castro in the original revolution and then stepped into the job of being Castro's personal assassin. He's a hero of the revolution. Which means he's got a free ticket to do pretty much whatever he wants. The police would cover up for him."

"And what will you do if he starts shooting?"

He glanced over at her blandly. "What do you think? I'll shoot back."

"Won't you end up in jail then?"

"I'm good. I would probably stand about a fifty-fifty chance of escaping the shooting scene." He shrugged. "As long as Camarillo's dead and you're safe, I'll do the jail time if they catch me. Uncle Sam would get me out in a year or two."

She blinked, stunned. He'd go to jail for her? She didn't know whether to think that was the sweetest thing anyone had ever said to her or whether it crossed the line into psychopathic. The danger of the man beside her struck her anew. He lived by an entirely different code than anything she'd ever encountered before. It was intensely attractive and every bit as frightening at the same time. Being with him was playing with fire. All that remained to be seen was just how badly he could burn her.

Mitch took a quick look up and down the deserted sidewalk and swerved without warning into a narrow alley. They picked their way past puddles and overflowing trash cans toward a single lightbulb dangling far in the bowels of the alley.

"The best social clubs in town, eh?" she muttered.

He grinned. "Patience, princess."

She followed him doubtfully to an unmarked door that looked made of solid steel. A totally clichéd little window slid open at eye level, and part of a man's face stared out at them. "*¿Sí?*" the guy grunted.

Mitch replied in rapid, fluent Cuban. Wow. Apparently he wasn't kidding when he said he'd been here before.

The little window closed and the sound of bolts being thrown came from behind the door. It swung open on a burst of color and music. Mitch's hand came to rest in the small of her back, sending lightning bolts shooting up and down her body. So distracted she could barely walk, she allowed him to guide her inside.

It was like stepping into a different world. The club's decor was tropical, full of greenery and vibrant colors. It was as unlike the city outside as a place could be. Live macaws perched on stands around the walls, lush palms and draped vines gave the place a jungle atmosphere, and the driving beat of a Latin band pulsed in the air.

Her Spanish was adequate to follow the conversation between Mitch and the maître d'. The Cuban was asking what their pleasure would be this evening.

"We'll be dining," Mitch replied. "Then maybe a little dancing."

The man nodded and led them through giant ferns and hanging bougainvilleas, past a dance floor full of bronze, gyrating flesh and to a separate dining room. Mitch indicated a table off to one side, but still in plain view of the other guests.

She slid into her seat and was startled when Mitch ordered rapidly for them without bothering to see a menu. Apparently he not only belonged to this place, but was a regular. The waiter nodded efficiently and left them alone.

"If you're worried about Camarillo shooting us, you couldn't have put us out in plainer sight for him to target," she murmured.

Mitch leaned across the glow of the candle, his face beautiful, his eyes deadly. He grasped her fingers and murmured back, "He would never show himself at a place like this. Most of the customers have mob or drug connections. If you take a casual look around, you'll see big, beefy guys at regular intervals all around the place. They're the house security staff. If anyone flashes a weapon in here, you'd better believe those guys would take them down before the first bullet flew."

"Then why are we here, if Camarillo wouldn't come here?"

"Because his friends would come here. If we show ourselves publicly enough, word will get back to him." A pause, and then he added, "This way we let him know we're here without direct danger to you."

She frowned. "Isn't going public with your presence in Cuba going to interfere with your main job of protecting Za—"

He pressed a finger against her lips. Smiling seductively for anyone who might be watching, he murmured, "Don't say it in here."

She nodded and smiled back her understanding.

He leaned back in his seat, playing with the stem of his wineglass. "It's a trade-off. You or You-know-who."

"But I'm not your job!" she exclaimed under her breath.

His mouth curved up. "Ahh, but you are. You're—" he glanced around quickly "—an important man's daughter, and you're in danger. It's definitely my job to protect you. Every last delicious inch of you."

Her breath caught at the sensual slide of his voice across her skin. She struggled to form rational thought. "But—" she frowned "—I'm supposed to be here to help you, not get in your way."

His golden gaze clouded over. "You're here to act as bait and leave as soon as we flush out our quarry. You're not a trained operative and I'm not about to put you in harm's way by expecting you to act like one."

"But I want to go in harm's way."

His fingers tightened almost painfully on hers. "Why's that? You've mentioned something to that effect before. What are you looking to get out of this?"

She mulled that one over for a moment and was saved from answering by the arrival of spinach, mango and strawberry salads. But as soon as she pushed her plate aside, Mitch's penetrating gaze was upon her again, pressing, probing, demanding answers.

"Well?" he prompted.

Persistent guy, darn it. She sighed. "I guess I'm looking for a little self-respect. I'm sick of being useless arm fluff."

His eyebrows shot up. He toyed with his wineglass again, twirling its delicate stem deftly between his strong fingers. "Seems to me that self-respect's not the problem," he finally commented.

"What do you mean?" It was her turn to stare at him, silently demanding answers.

He spoke carefully. "You strike me as having plenty of self-esteem. I think your self-image is just fine. Which leads me to believe you're mainly interested in gaining someone else's respect. Who are you trying to impress?"

She squirmed beneath his all too seeing gaze. Who indeed?

"Your father?"

She scowled. "I gave up on impressing him a long time ago. He'll always see me as his helpless little girl and there's not a thing I can do about it."

Mitch nodded contemplatively. "The ex-fiancé, then?"

Kinsey gasped, stunned. He knew about that? She'd so hoped her humiliation would fade away, eclipsed by some other celebrity scandal. Mitch was an undercover agent for goodness' sake! How had he come across those damned pictures? Her face heated up. She was probably the same color as her dress.

Mitch frowned. "There's no need to be embarrassed. You're not the one who put the pictures on the Web. Your ex should be ashamed of himself. And if I do say so myself, you're an incredibly beautiful woman. I suspect you photograph a whole lot better than most celebrities who get caught topless."

"Yeah, but it pretty much blows me ever being the kind of girl a nice guy wants to bring home to meet the parents. Nothing like Googling the girlfriend and having her pop up on the Internet in all her glory."

"Is that what you're upset about? You think nice guys won't be interested in you anymore?"

She frowned. When he put it like that, it did sound kind of lame.

"Any decent guy would understand that you were taken advantage of. He wouldn't blame you."

"Would you want a girl who millions of men had seen topless?" she accused.

"As long as she was loyal to me, I wouldn't care. The human body is no big deal. But cheating on someone—" he broke off, his expression blacker than she'd ever seen it before.

Into his heavy silence, she murmured, pleasantly, "Your casual attitude about nudity is refreshingly… European." She wasn't entirely sure she believed him, though. What man didn't get possessive of his woman? Especially an aggressively alpha male like Mitch? She spied the murderous look in his eye and nodded to herself. Yup, his expression was at distinct odds with his words.

Or perhaps that murderous look in his eyes had something to do with his remark about cheating women? Had someone cheated on him? What woman in her right mind would step out on a man like Mitch Perovski if they'd actually landed him? The idea of Mitch giving her his unreserved affection took her breath away, as improbable as it was captivating to imagine.

As she turned over possible ways to probe him about his past love life without him growling her off the subject, Mitch seemed to shake off his grim thoughts and took a sip of his wine. He grinned over at her, back to his usual careless self. "Who wants a nice guy anyway? We rogues are more fun."

She met his smiling gaze with a teasing one of her own. "I'm a spoiled jet-set baby, you know. I've partied with some pretty hard-core fun-seekers in my day. Are you sure you can cut it with me?"

He leaned forward, blatantly looking down her dress. "I'll do my best."

Her chest abruptly felt like it was on fire, throbbing and swollen beneath his incendiary gaze. Her nipples puckered up hard and sensitive, her dress rubbing almost painfully against them.

His gaze lifted to hers, knowing. Satisfied. *Smug.* She laughed helplessly. "You're incorrigible."

Grinning, he lifted his glass to her in silent toast.

The meal was as spicy and colorful as the club, and Kinsey savored every bite. Of course, part of the seasoning was the nonverbal exchange between her and Mitch as he watched her eat. She'd never thought of it as a particularly sexual experience to eat in front of a man, but she was abruptly aware of the smooth slide of the silverware against her lips, the texture and bite of the food on her tongue, the smoky heat of her prime rib and the tingly chill of the champagne. The chocolate mousse he ordered for their dessert was like sex on a spoon, smooth and rich and sensual. She'd eaten at some of the best restaurants on earth in her day, but never had she enjoyed a meal as much as this one.

They small-talked for a while after the meal, letting their food settle and establishing their cover as intimate acquaintances. Eventually, Mitch murmured, "Shall we dance?"

She glanced over at the dance floor. She'd spent plenty of time in jet-set discos and was a fair dancer, but the way the Cuban women were moving to the hot, salsa rhythms was a little intimidating. Nonetheless, she smiled over at him and stood up. He took her hand and led her out onto the floor.

She needn't have worried. The music and the moment took hold of her and moved her body for her. Mitch's golden gaze dared her to let go, to meet him halfway. And safely surrounded by a wall of perspiring, gyrating bodies, she did just that. She threw her head back, closed her eyes, and let the music roll through her.

Mitch took advantage of every gaze in the joint being riveted on Kinsey to scope out the patrons. She was obviously a trained dancer and moved with a lithe fluidity that made sweat pop out on his forehead. She seemed to be having that effect on a lot of men.

He recognized a number of the usual suspects—local criminal bosses, smugglers, and a few midlevel drug traffickers. What he didn't see were the top-level government officials and high rollers Camarillo ran with. Damn.

He let the locals get an eyeful of Kinsey, then he gathered her close to his side, laying definite and aggressive claim to her as he escorted her, flushed and laughing, from the dance floor.

"That was fun," she proclaimed. "I want to dance some more."

He grinned. The princess was surprisingly uninhibited when she let her hair down. "How 'bout I take you to the hottest band in Cuba?"

"Lead on, good sir."

He looked down at her. She shone as brightly as the sun, joy bursting forth from deep within her to illuminate her whole being. Ahh, to dive into that light, to lose himself in it, to chase away the darkness in his soul...

She was not for him. Not her innocence, not her agenda to prove herself to her ex-fiancé or her father or whoever pushed her buttons. She was merely playing at being a spy and looked like she thought this was all some elaborate James Bond game. She wouldn't be shining so brightly when she had to live in constant fear, or run for her life. Or when she came face to face with death. He sure as hell didn't want to be the one to introduce her to the dark side of night.

But deep in his heart, he had a sinking feeling he

would be the one to do just that. This mission had blood written all over it.

His pleasure sapped out of the moment, he took Kinsey's elbow and guided her out of the club. "C'mon. Time to throw our line into a bigger pond."

This time he drove them out to the island's north shore and its casino strip, Little Las Vegas. He pulled in at an exclusive hotel and handed over the cruiser's keys to a valet. He took possession of Kinsey from the bell captain who'd solicitously helped her out of the car, and they strolled into the lobby. He made a point of ignoring the unobtrusive surveillance cameras sprinkled more thickly than any regular hotel warranted. With a nod to the concierge, he led Kinsey confidently through the lobby and back to the beachside casino.

She didn't act impressed by the assault of flashing lights, jumbled neon colors, and noise as they stepped onto the gaming floor. But then, she'd probably been to the swankiest casinos in the world already. Being around a woman like her could seriously deflate a guy's ego. Good thing he had no ego. He was a sewer rat, a creature of the night, and he had no illusions to the contrary.

They approached an unmarked door near the back of the casino. It was remarkable only for the burly guard lounging casually on a bar stool beside it.

"Private gambling parlor?" Kinsey murmured.

"Nope. That band I promised you," he muttered back.

They stepped up to the guard, and Mitch nodded. In quiet Cuban, he dropped the right names and words into a few sentences. The guard looked Kinsey up and down appreciatively, and Mitch gritted his teeth. This was exactly what she was here for. No amount of money could pay for the legitimacy she gave his cover. No sewer rat could land a woman like her in a million years. Even in a sleazy little red dress, she radiated so much class it dripped from her. If the entry passwords happened to have changed since he was last here, Mitch would give it better than even money the guard would let them in anyway just because Kinsey looked so damn good.

For whatever reason, the guard reached out and keyed a rapid number sequence on a wall-mounted security pad. A green light came on over the number pad and the guy gave the door handle a tug. With a smarmy smile for Kinsey, the guy let them in. Mitch hung on tightly to his right fist, which seemed to have developed an alarming need to bury itself in the guard's leering face.

And then they were inside. While the last place had been as much restaurant as anything else, this place was primarily a dance club. The music was loud, the dance floor dominating the two-story space.

"Wow. Good-looking clientele," Kinsey commented.

He cast a glance at the row of unattached women artfully draped on bar stools around the margins of the room. "Hookers," he bit out.

Kinsey threw him a startled look. "Will the men in here think I'm one, too?"

Mitch grinned down at her. "Honey, there's not a man alive who could look at you and see a hooker. You're a princess from the top of your head to the tip of your toes."

"Thanks, I think."

His smile widened. "It's a compliment. Besides, I'm not leaving your side for a second in here. No other man's getting a shot at you. You're taken."

"Who all is here?"

Mitch didn't spare a glance for the male clientele. He already knew who they were. "Government types. Management tier guys in organized crime rings. Businessmen looking to grease palms."

"Sounds like an unsavory lot."

"You hang onto that thought, princess. Don't mess with these guys. They'd chew you up and spit you out."

She pursed her lips. "I don't know about that. They can't be much worse than politicians and lobbyists. Or, heaven forbid, social climbers."

"Good point. Can I get you a drink?"

"Sure."

He guided her over to the bar and shouted in Cuban to the bartender to be heard over the blaring Latin-disco fusion music. Two condensation-covered glasses were forthcoming momentarily. He handed the red-orange one with the umbrella to Kinsey while he took the clear one.

She took a sip and nodded her approval. She leaned close to shout in his ear, "How did you know what I'd like?"

He turned his head, putting his mouth practically on her ear. "My Chicks 101 class, freshman year of college. Fastest way to get girls drunk and frisky is to feed 'em fruity rum drinks they can suck down like Kool-Aid."

"Frisky, eh?" Her eyes sparkled with laughter. God, he'd love to bottle all that brilliance, then guzzle it until he was completely drunk on it. "Since I seem to have missed How to Pick Up Guys 101 in college, what're you drinking?"

"Water."

"Water?" she echoed, surprised.

He leaned even closer, dropping a light kiss on her neck, just below her ear. She gasped as obvious sexual vibes rattled through her. He was all kinds of happy to share his suffering of that ilk with her. Belatedly, he murmured, "I never mix alcohol and firearms."

Watching her unfocused gaze, it clearly took a moment for his words to sink in. He smiled to himself. So responsive, his princess.

"You're armed?" she mumbled back, alarmed. "How'd you get through the metal detectors?"

He grinned and replied conversationally, "Did you know they make ceramics these days that are stronger than steel and more heat-resistant?"

She considered that for a moment. "So, I can pretty much forget feeling safe on an airplane ever again?"

He laughed. "Nah, you're okay most of the time."

"Maybe if you were there to handle anything that came up. After this is over, can I hire you to fly with me everywhere I go?"

Their gazes met. Blue melted into gold. He murmured, "I'll fly anywhere with you, princess."

"I'll hold you to that," she murmured back.

"You do that."

The music shifted into a slow, sexy ballad of love and loss, spurned lovers and heartbreak. But the melody spoke of smoky nights and unbearable passion. The ocean pounded outside and the muggy air made tendrils curl around Kinsey's face, accentuating her beauty even more. He shouldn't do it but had to get his hands on her.

"Dance with me," he murmured.

Without a word, she laid her hand in his and followed him out to the dance floor. The lights were turned down, the singer wailing for her lover to come back. He drew Kinsey to him, sighing in pleasure as her slender body gently pressed against his, absorbing his hard angles and power into her softness. It was like coming home. So right. So perfect. Her fingers played with the short hair at the back of his neck, her thigh rubbing gently between his. In heels, she was only a few inches shorter than him and her cheek rested against his neck. A single thought filled his brain, crowding out mission and duty until he could form only a single burning sentence. *He needed her.*

They swayed together like that until the singer's voice rose in an angry anthem to swearing off lovers forever and the song ended. He snorted mentally. How very dramatic.

Kinsey lifted her head off his shoulder but did not step away from him. She murmured into his ear, "We've attracted some attention."

"Honey, you've attracted all kinds of attention."

"I'm talking about the pair of men in black suits at the table by the window. East end of the room. They don't look any too happy to have spotted you."

Kinsey's words jolted him like a bucket of ice water to the face. Work. The mission. Both missions. Which sharks had taken the bait first? Camarillo's men or Zaragosa's?

Chapter 8

"Let's go for a walk."

The grim tone in Mitch's voice jolted Kinsey out of the magical haze enveloping her. Regret for the loss of his strong arms around her, his hard body cradling hers, stabbed her.

She sighed. "Is this walk for business or pleasure?"

"All business." He smiled down at her suggestively, his voice entirely grim under the sexy expression.

Taking her cue from him, she leaned into him, draping her arms around his neck wantonly, and flashing him her best seductive smile. "Shall we, then?"

He reached up to untangle her arms, kissing her fingertips as he set her away from him. "C'mon. Let's make these guys earn their paychecks."

She was surprised when he led her toward the back of the dance club and not the door they'd come in by.

But then she spied another exit leading out to the beach. A bouncer/guard nodded to them as they stepped outside into the muggy night. Salt hung thick and warm in the air and she could all but feel her hair frizzing up.

"This way," Mitch bit out.

Drat. He was back in full-blown work mode. They moved quickly across a flagstone patio and toward the sand.

She stopped at the step-down onto the beach. "Just a second. I have to take my shoes off." He frowned, and she added, "I can move a lot faster this way. Besides, it helps maintain our cover of being lovers to walk barefoot in the sand."

"You learn fast. Let's go."

They stripped off their shoes and then slogged off through the sand, running toward the beach. She laughed brightly like it was actually fun, while cursing Mitch for making her do this. Perspiration popped out on her forehead. Good thing she wore waterproof mascara and not much other makeup.

They stopped at the edge of the ocean, the waves just lapping over their toes. Mitch startled her by sweeping her up into his arms. "Look over my shoulder and tell me if you see any men who've just come outside."

"Yeah. A pair of them."

He swore under his breath. Against her lips he muttered, "Off to my right, there are a series of cliffs and sand dunes. We're going to head for those and see who follows. Stay just at the edge of the water. The sand is firmest there and gives the best footing."

"Two more men just stepped outside," she announced.

"Are they talking to the first pair?"

"Nope. If anything the two pairs look to be avoiding each other."

"Hmm. Interesting. Let's go."

Interesting? They had no less than four thugs commencing tailing them and he thought it was *interesting?* She'd hate to see what made him nervous. They took off at a jog, holding hands. He laughed at her, his gaze as grim and bleak as the black ocean behind him. She laughed back, worry no doubt shining back in her gaze.

Mitch led her along the beach until a series of rock outcroppings and undulating crests of sand rose on their right. The beach took a sharp turn, and the second they rounded the headland, Mitch swerved inland fast.

"Stay on the rocks," he hissed. "We can't leave footprints in the sand."

They leaped and skipped like mountain goats across the rocks. Her feet burned from the rough stone, but something in the urgent set of Mitch's shoulders kept her from complaining. They climbed for maybe a minute and then, without warning, Mitch grabbed her arm and yanked her down into a crouch beside him. She looked back toward the beach and their pursuers, and was startled to see how high up they were. It was probably thirty feet down to the water's edge.

"What are we doing?" she whispered.

"Seeing who's motivated enough to follow us."

In another minute, the first pair of men burst around the headland at a full run. They paused, obviously searching for her and Mitch. She started to duck, but Mitch grabbed her arm and muttered under the muted roar of the ocean, "Don't move."

The two men ran on.

After they'd gone and the crash of waves was all that remained, Mitch murmured, "In conditions this dark, they'd have to be right on top of us to see our faces. But, they can still pick out movement at a distance. When you're hiding, standing still is more important than being out of sight."

"Who were they?"

"Given the high-quality suits, the short hair, and the general bearing, I'd say they're government."

"Why would they follow you?"

"They're likely part of the faction that wants Zaragosa eliminated, and they know the U.S. will send in someone like me to watch his back. I'm a known American operator in certain government circles. As soon as they spotted me, they would've followed me."

"With the intent to do what?" she asked in alarm.

"Get me out of the way so they can take out Zaragosa."

"As in kill you?" she squawked.

He shrugged. "It's all right. Now that I've seen their faces, I know who to go after myself. I'll capture one of those guys and find out who he works for. Or, if neither of them will cooperate, it won't be that hard to get names on them after they're eliminated and find out who they're aligned with. I'll have that faction cleaned up in a few weeks."

He sounded awfully confident of his ability to casually take out a whole group of well-connected and probably well-protected people. Her father had warned her. But still the question entered her mind. How dangerous *was* Mitch, anyway?

She glanced down at the beach. "We'd better be still again because here come two more guys."

Mitch froze beside her, predatory focus pouring off him. It was like crouching beside a tiger, seconds before it sprang for the kill. The moment was dangerous. Thrilling. A second pair of men paused as they rounded the headland, searching the way the first pair had. Their faces turned up toward the cliffs, and Mitch hissed on an indrawn breath. He must recognize them. She studied the two men's faces as carefully as she could in the scant light, memorizing their features. Who knew if she'd recognize them in the light of day, but it was worth a try. This pair was more casually dressed than the first pair, both wearing white cotton shirts untucked over dark slacks. Their hair was longer, and their general demeanor less disciplined than the first men. She'd lay odds these guys were not Cuban government.

The men took off in a jog, moving on down the beach.

"Who were they?" she ventured to whisper. With the ocean below, she could probably have shouted safely, but Mitch's hunting alertness seemed to call for whispers.

"Camarillo's men. I've run into the taller one before."

And it didn't sound like that had been a friendly meeting. Mitch's voice dripped with contained violence.

"Now what?" she asked.

"Now we wait."

"For what?"

They'll come back this way eventually. Their cars are back at the casino. Once they've given up the chase, we'll turn the tables and follow them."

"Which pair are you going to follow?"

He turned his gaze on her, frustration glinting in it. "That's a good question."

"Too bad we can't split up and each take one pair," she tossed out.

Mitch reacted violently. "No way. You're not leaving my side until we take out Camarillo and those two down on the beach." He paused, and then added, "I guess that settles that. We go after Camarillo's flunkies and hope they lead us to him."

And then what? Her brain knew Mitch intended to kill Camarillo, but now that the reality of it was one step nearer, cold dread formed a knot in her stomach.

How long they waited up on that cliff, she wasn't sure. Long enough to relax a bit. Long enough to be aware of Mitch's contained power against her right side. Long enough to start fantasizing about turning to him and kissing him to distraction, stretching out on the sand beside him and making love in the shadow of the ocean's majesty. Long enough for Mitch's jaw, and then his whole body to go tight, and for him to glance over at her and mutter, "You can stop that now."

"Stop what?" she asked, startled.

"You think I can't feel what's going on in your head?"

Her eyebrows shot straight up. "You're psychic, too?"

"No, dammit, I'm a man." And with that, he leaned over, grabbed the back of her neck and dragged her forward to meet him—not that he had to force the issue all that hard. She leaned into him eagerly, seeking the fire within him, reveling in the leashed violence of the man.

He whispered, "And you're a woman with sex on her mind."

Their mouths collided, tongues tangling, hands

seeking, bodies straining toward one another. He growled deep in the back of his throat, a call of need that reached right inside her. She turned on her knees to face him fully and flung herself against the wall of muscle and strength that was Mitch. His powerful arms caught her up against him, wrapping her in safety and desire. The combination enflamed her beyond all reason.

"Make love to me," she murmured against his mouth.

"Don't tempt me," he muttered back.

"I'm not tempting you," she declared, "I mean it. Right here. Right now."

He lifted his mouth away from hers, his eyes glittering, an eerie glow in the blackness of the night. "Not here. Not now. There are four armed and dangerous men down there, hunting us."

Disappointment speared into her. He must've seen it because he added, his lips moving against her neck, "Don't knock it. Sand and sex don't mix. If you want to make love, try me somewhere with no gunmen and no sand on the floor." As if to soften his rebuff, he nibbled his way along her shoulder until goose bumps popped out on her sensitized flesh.

She took his head in both her hands and lifted it until she could look into his eyes. "Do you mean that?"

His gaze flickered in hesitation. "You understand what I do, right?"

She nodded.

"And you understand that my job forces me to travel. A lot."

She nodded again.

"I'll leave for months on end and you'll never hear from me."

"Yes, yes, I know all that."

He shook his head. "You hear me, but you don't really get what I'm saying. I *will* walk out on you. Even if we make mind-blowing, passionate, addictive love, I'll still leave. Maybe I'll come back from the next mission and maybe I won't."

She frowned. He was talking like, if they made love, they had to commit to one another forever. She wasn't at all sure she wanted forever with anyone. Not after the garbage her last boyfriend had pulled on her. "Mitch, I'm not looking for 2.5 kids and a white picket fence. I want you and you want me. Why does it have to be any more complicated than that?"

"Because women always want more. They start wanting something casual, and before you know it, they're looking for rings and I do's. I'm not opposed to making love with you, just as long as you understand that nothing between us is going to override my work. It comes first. It's nothing personal against you, mind you." He gestured down the cliff at the beach where they awaited four killers. "This is what I do. It's who I am."

She glanced down at the deserted surf. "I understand that."

"No. You don't. You have no idea what I really do and who I really am. You still think this is some expanded, live-action version of a James Bond movie."

"James Bond kills people."

"Yes, and it's all bloodless and clean and cut-and-dried in the movies. I assure you. Real life isn't that way at all."

Okay, so maybe she didn't understand what he was trying to tell her. Maybe because he didn't have the words to convey it, or maybe because she had no frame of reference in which to comprehend his comments. And yet, she still wanted him. With every molecule in her body.

So, he only wanted a casual fling. Wasn't that exactly what she wanted, too? Was it a selfish thing with her? Was he a new toy she had to have for herself, or was there more to this attraction burning up the night between them? Would she be able to walk away from him? To let him walk away from her?

"Someone's coming," he murmured suddenly.

In an instant, the potential lover was gone, replaced by the panther, a great predatory cat stalking in the blackest night. His stillness was instant and complete, his intensity palpable in the air between them. Slowly, she turned her gaze to look down at the beach below. The government men. Kinsey frowned. How had they gotten in front of Camarillo's men? Had the pairs of men passed each other on the narrow beach? The way they'd avoided acknowledging each other back on the porch at the dance club, she found it hard to believe they'd walked past each other casually out here on a fifteen-foot wide strip of sand.

Mitch must've had the same thought, for the second the government men passed out of sight below, he whirled around to look inland. She did the same, scanning the featureless undulations of the sand behind them. He thought Camarillo's thugs were out there. How would they ever spot the men?

"C'mon," Mitch whispered.

She followed him down the jagged outcropping. Crouching uncomfortably low, they made their way along the margin of the rocks and sand, gazing out into the undulating dunes for…something…some sign of their other two pursuers.

When her legs were screaming in so much pain she didn't think she could go another step, Mitch paused in the shadow of an overhang. Thankfully, he stood up straight. She nearly cried in relief as blood returned to her cramped thighs.

"Isn't it dangerous to stand up like this?" she breathed.

"With the rocks at our backs and overhead, our silhouettes won't be visible to anyone looking this way."

She nodded, too relieved to care if they were exposed or not.

But then he stepped near and her breath hitched in her throat. His left arm went around her waist, drawing her close. He put his mouth on her ear, and over the shiver that raced through her, he whispered, "Watch for movement. A head popping up over the line of a dune, a fall of sand, a shadow moving where it shouldn't. They're out there. I can feel it."

She nodded her understanding. Hidden under the overhang, they stood still, searching for their quarry. It didn't take long. Off to their left, she spotted something breaking the wavy line of a dune crest. It was round and dark. A human head.

She gripped Mitch's elbow tightly and pointed to where the man's head had been a moment before. She held up one finger. Mitch nodded. They studied the area just ahead of her sighting, waiting for the men to show themselves again.

Camarillo's men must realize how dangerous Mitch was, for they, too, were moving with extreme caution. They didn't show themselves again. It was only by an abrupt whoosh of sand as a dune crest collapsed that Mitch and Kinsey got an inkling of the men's position. Kinsey started. It was only two dunes over, maybe fifty feet away. No more.

Mitch yanked her down and took off crawling back the way they'd come. It was murder moving on her hands and knees, scraping both on the rough rock and then grinding sand into the raw flesh. But murder was the operative word. She got the distinct impression that she and Mitch would be murdered if they didn't get out of there and fast. After a few minutes of excruciating crawling, he stopped and eased back into a narrow cleft in the rock face.

They had to squeeze in tight together to fit, and it put them body to body in a way that left very little to the imagination.

"They're coming after us," Mitch breathed. "Take this."

Something cold and heavy pressed into her hand. She recognized the rough grip against her palm. A gun. From hunter back to hunted, were they? "You keep that," she whispered urgently. "You need it a whole lot more than I do. Besides, you know how to use it."

"I have another one. Two more, in fact. That has nine shots and the safety's off. Point and shoot. Got it?"

She nodded, alarmed. There was something very, very not James Bond about holding a loaded gun in her hand.

"You stay here. I'm going out there."

"But I thought we were going to follow them to Camarillo…."

"Change of plans. They're endangering you. I'm not playing games with your life. I'll be back in a while. Don't come out until I come back for you, or daylight."

Daylight? That was hours away! She started when he dropped a quick hard kiss on her mouth. And then he was gone. She slid farther back into the crack and realized the back of it was not entirely vertical. By scrambling up a series of easy footholds, she was able to climb up high enough to see much of the field of sand below.

It didn't take her long to spot Camarillo's men. Their white shirts were easy to see against the gray sand. Mitch's black clothing ought to be equally easy to spot, but she had a hard time picking him out. Finally she realized she was looking right at him, but he'd taken off his shirt. His bronze skin blended in beautifully with the sand. She tried to keep him in sight, but he was just too good and she lost him. She took stock of the white-shirted men. Uh-oh. They'd split up. One was circling wide to their right while the other went left. What were they up to?

And then she stared in shock. Three more pale shapes were moving stealthily across the sand. Oh, no! Camarillo's men had called in reinforcements! Mitch was out there alone against five men! She had to warn him. But how?

She scrambled down the cleft and moved forward to the edge of the dunes. The last time she saw him, Mitch was off to her left at about a forty-five degree angle. She headed that way, her ankles sinking deeply in the sand with every frantic step. She tried to run, but only managed a clumsy shamble. She approached the first ridge. She lay down and rolled over it the way she'd seen Mitch do from her perch in the cleft. Then she tumbled to her feet, ignoring the sand sticking to her skin, and was off half running, half sliding down the lee face of the dune.

She could almost feel the three men closing in from her right and the fourth man from behind. The net grew tighter and tighter around her until she felt choked. Or maybe that was just panic squeezing her throat so tight. Up another dune, roll across its peak, and slide on her behind down its steep face. *Hang on, Mitch.*

And then she heard a noise that made her blood run cold. A metallic spit. If television had the sound effect right, that was the sound of a silenced pistol firing. Oh, God. Mitch!

She abandoned all attempt at stealth and sprinted for where she estimated he'd be. One, maybe two more ridges over. She scrambled up the next ridge. Threw herself flat on her belly. Flung herself into a roll over the crest.

And pulled up short with the round, deadly bore of a gun in her face.

Chapter 9

Kinsey jolted as Mitch jerked the weapon up and away from her.

"What in bloody hell are you doing out here?" he growled under his breath.

"There are five men, now."

"What? Where?"

She gave him her best guess as to where the men were. Which was to say, they were surrounded.

Mitch talked low and fast. "I think I hit the guy on the far left already, but he's probably not out of action. Maybe I slowed him down, though. Let's move toward him before these bastards close in on us and shoot us like fish in a barrel. Stay right behind me. And if you can, keep an eye out behind us."

It was awkward going, scrambling on all fours behind Mitch and trying to look over her shoulder pe-

riodically. She was sweaty, covered in sand, and scared
to death. Her hands and knees hurt, her arms ached fe-
rociously, and she was out of breath. But Mitch kept
going in front of her, and she pushed on doggedly, her
hair hanging in her face and generally getting in the
way. So much for glamorous shoot-outs on yachts and
the patios of casinos in evening gowns and tuxedos.

Mitch flopped onto his belly in front of her without
warning. Two bright flashes of light came from his
clenched fists. *Spit. Spit.*

He'd just shot at someone. Mitch took off crawling
again. Did he hit the guy? She didn't dare stop long
enough to ask.

She glanced back over her shoulder and gasped in
alarm. Two men were just topping a tall ridge, two
dunes back. Mitch must've heard her, for he ordered in
a bare whisper, "Get down!"

She flattened herself instantly in the sand, getting it
in her mouth and nose. Mitch's arm came across her
back. "This way."

He reversed direction, crawling back up the steep,
downwind ridge they'd just slid down. It was hard work.
Her hands and feet slid almost as far back down as she
reached up with every movement. But after scrambling
madly for several harrowing seconds, she came up
beside Mitch, who crouched just below the ridge.

He put his mouth directly on her ear. "When I say
go, pop up beside me and shoot at the nearest guy to
you. Understand?"

He wanted her to *shoot* at someone? She stared at
him in shock.

"We're way outgunned, here. I need you. Remember

what I showed you on the boat? Hold the gun in both hands, point at the guy's belly and pull the trigger."

Numbly, she nodded. She realized her knees—and hands—were shaking violently. She wasn't going to hit anything if she didn't get control of herself. But to *shoot* someone? What if she missed? Would she and Mitch both die? The thought dissolved the last of her control.

And then Mitch tensed beside her. By main force, she pushed her senses past her panic, past the roaring of blood in her ears, past the pounding of her pulse in her chest and temples. And heard what had made Mitch tighten up, preparing to spring. A noise. Just on the other side of the dune. Ohmigosh. Their pursuers couldn't be more than fifteen or twenty feet away. At least that solved the question of how she was possibly going to hit these guys. They were too close for her to miss.

And then, before she had any more time to fall apart, Mitch glanced over at her. Mouthed the word, "Ready?"

For lack of anything else to do, she nodded. It was that or run screaming.

He waited one more heartbeat, and then murmured, "Go."

She stood up by reflex, bringing the pistol up in front of her as Mitch did the same with two pistols, one in either hand. She jumped violently when she spotted a man no more than ten feet from her, coming up the dune face fast.

She didn't even take time to aim. She just pulled the trigger. A huge explosion of noise rocked her as the heavy weapon kicked up violently in her hand. The man in front of her staggered. Stopped.

She stared in utter horror at the red mass that had been his face just a moment ago. He tottered. Fell backward like a tree. Rolled back down the slope. Came to a stop at the bottom of the dune.

"Get down!" Mitch yelled, spinning to their rear.

She dropped to her knees and swiveled around. Two round heads popped up over the ridge behind them.

"Jump!" Mitch shouted.

He didn't give her any more instruction than that, but she needed none. They leaped as one for the ridge at their backs and its scant protection from the gunmen in front of her.

She landed half on top of something warm and squishy. The sand was cool and wet under her hands. Black in the scant light. It smelled sharp. She turned her head. Protruding, glassy eyes stared at her, sand sticking to their unblinking surface. She jerked back with a scream.

More flashes from beside her and she realized Mitch was firing again.

Her stomach rumbling with nausea, she dragged her attention to the firefight blazing around her. There was practically no sound, just sand flying and the spit of silenced bullets in the pauses between waves breaking on the shore behind them.

She tried to peer over the ridge, tried to take aim on the men shooting at them, but she couldn't see anything in the dark, and there was no way she was hitting what tiny little target one of the shooters might give her in a careless moment. Helplessly, she watched on. And then Mitch flung one of the pistols away and shifted the remaining weapon to his right hand.

"I'm getting low on ammo. Bring me that guy's gun." He jerked his head at the body below. The man she'd shot.

Obediently, she scrambled down the slope. She tugged on the dead man's shoulder. Lord, he was heavy. She moved around his other side to heave him onto his back. And stared, appalled, at the damage she'd wrought to another human being. His nose and upper jaw were mostly gone. Teeth perched in bloody gore that used to be his lower jaw, and one of his eye sockets had ruptured, leaving the eyeball hanging by several stringy nerves and veins beside his left ear. She dropped to her knees and retched in the sand.

"Hurry!" Mitch called from above.

Swiping at her mouth with the back of her hand, she jerked the gun out of the dead man's rubbery fingers. Nearly sick again, she turned away and headed back up to Mitch's position. He held his hand out the moment she arrived beside him, and she slapped the weapon into his palm. In one motion he drew the weapon forward, aimed and fired.

She flinched at the muzzle flash and crawled over to the dead man on their right to scavenge his gun as well. Fortunately, this guy had fallen with his gun hand outstretched, and she left the body where it was. She snatched the gun and passed it to Mitch as well. There was only one more dead guy and her weapon, and then they'd be out of ammo. Then what were they going to do?

Mitch apparently was thinking about that very same thing. As he reached for the third gun she passed him, he muttered, "We're getting the hell out of here. Start back toward the casino. Head for the beach, then run back to the club. I'll meet you at the car."

"What are you going to do?"

"I've had enough of these bastards. I'm going to kill them."

She didn't stop to ask how. She just started to retreat. She averted her gaze as she passed the man she'd shot, but it didn't matter. The sight of what she'd done to him was burned into her memory forever. As she topped the next ridge, she looked back. Mitch was just turning to follow her. He nodded reassuringly. And then it was a mad scramble, first over the dunes to the beach, and then a dead sprint along the blessedly firm sand. She'd almost arrived back at the hotel when she heard footsteps behind her. Mitch. She stopped gratefully, and turned to wait for him.

And jerked in shock as a beefy, dark-haired man closed in on her. Belatedly, she remembered the gun in her hand and raised it to shoot. He was almost upon her. She braced herself to pull the trigger, when another shape came hurtling out of the darkness from her right. In a flying tackle, the second man took out her attacker.

The two men rolled over and over in the sand, carrying them into the shallow surf. They struggled fiercely, and she couldn't make out anything but foam and sand and body parts. And then one of the men rose up over the other one, straddling his chest for a moment. A slash of dull metal, and the man on the bottom's throat exploded like a swollen sausage sliced open. The white, fibrous tube of an esophagus burst out, along with the dark, slimy strands of veins. Blood went everywhere.

She staggered back in terror, aiming her pistol at the dark form that rose away from the dead man and whirled to face her.

Mitch.

She leaped forward, flinging herself into his disheveled arms. "Are there any more of them?" she gasped.

"Nope. He was the last one. You're safe now."

And that was all it took for the shaking to set in. She'd seen more horror tonight than she needed in a lifetime. Somewhere in the aftermath she started to sob, and Mitch urged her face down to his chest to muffle the sound. But then he held her tight and let her cry it out.

How long they stood there like that, red waves washing up over their feet as the dead man bled out behind them, she had no idea. But finally, Mitch murmured into her hair, "We've got to get out of here, princess."

She nodded numbly against his chest and let him lead her around the casino and directly to the parking lot. He put her into the passenger seat of their car then went around and got in the driver's side.

She noticed his hands were steady and sure on the steering wheel as he guided the vehicle into the last vestiges of the night. Just another day at the office for him. Kill four men in cold blood and leave them for the vultures. Of course, her hands weren't clean, either. The destroyed visage of the man she'd shot haunted her, leering at her, a macabre reminder of her night's work.

Dawn was just breaking as they returned to their hotel. There was blood on her dress, but the red stain wasn't tremendously obvious against the scarlet background. Mitch hustled her past a sleepy clerk and up to their room.

"Why don't you take a shower, Kinsey?" he murmured quietly. "I've got to make a phone call."

To report his kills? Did they keep some sort of scoreboard back in the H.O.T. Watch ops center? Score four for Mitch Perovski, and one for the rookie, Kinsey Hollingsworth. She shuddered at the thought. "Am I a criminal now?"

She must have voiced the thought aloud, for Mitch responded gently, "No, you clearly acted in self-defense. No court would convict you, not in the United States or Cuba."

"But I killed a man."

"A man who would have killed you in another second or so. It was you or him. You did the right thing. Now go take that shower. A hot one. You'll feel better, I promise."

Mitch waited until the water was running in the bathroom to dial the ops center. "Lancer here."

Brady Hathaway picked up the line. "Looks like you had some excitement last night. We had you on satellite. Picked up quite a few muzzle flashes down there. You two okay?"

"Yeah. Five hostiles down, by the way. A mixed bag. Several of Camarillo's men, possibly a couple of *federales*."

"How's your girl?"

"Pretty shook up. She shot a guy in the face at point-blank range. Killed him."

Hathaway didn't comment. Both men knew what it was like to experience a first kill. Kinsey would have to work it out in her own way. No one could make it better for her. "Don't let her crash and burn too hard, eh?" Hathaway finally murmured.

"I'll do what I can."

"What are your plans now?"

"I got a knife to the throat of one of the guys before I killed him. He gave me an address where I can find Camarillo. Thought I might go pay him a little visit this evening."

"Do you want to wait for backup? I can have a team in-country in twenty-four hours."

Mitch considered. Common sense said to wait for a half-dozen of his colleagues and the extra gear they'd bring with them, but his gut said to take action immediately to keep Kinsey safe. "I'd better hit him before he has time to get ready for an assault. I'll take this one on my own."

"Don't make it personal, Lancer. This is business. Just business."

"I hear you." He might hear the words, but that didn't mean he agreed with them. This was personal. Camarillo's men had nearly succeeded at killing Kinsey. Payback was required. Now.

"Did you get pictures of your attackers?" Hathaway asked, jarring Mitch out of his grim thoughts.

"With my cell phone camera. They're dead in the photos, but maybe you can make ID's anyway. I'll send them to you as soon as we hang up."

"Roger. We'll get on it."

"Start with the database of Camarillo's henchmen."

"Will do. Get some rest. And take care of your girl."

Hathaway hung up. Mitch sent the pictures wirelessly to the ops center. And then, finally, he relaxed. He let the stark terror of the night flow over him and out of him. Damn, that had been close. Way, way too close. Thank God Kinsey had come out and warned him about the additional men. Without that, and the extra firepower she'd provided, it could've been dicey. Well, he'd wanted her to get over the James Bond fantasy. For better or worse, she'd seen the real deal now.

He swore under his breath. It had been fun while it lasted having a woman as beautiful and sexy as Kinsey chasing after him. He'd even let himself indulge in a fantasy of the two of them being together. But after tonight—

Now she knew him for the killer he was. It was one thing to shoot at some guys on a speedboat. But to order her to shoot a guy's face off…then to slit a guy's throat right in front of her…

She'd never look at him the same way again. James Bond was dead. Mitch got up heavily and went over to the small refrigerator. He pulled out two minibottles of whiskey and opened them. Grasping both bottles in his right hand, he tossed them back in one slug. The dark liquor burned a path through his gut but didn't do a thing to unwind the giant knot of tension at the base of his skull. He opened the refrigerator again. Stared at the rows of little bottles. Slammed the door shut without taking out any more booze.

Dammit, he'd really wanted her for himself.

Chapter 10

Kinsey hugged the hotel's thick, complimentary bathrobe more tightly around her and headed for the window. She'd slept away most of the day. Her dreams had been bloody, and she felt intolerably soiled by them. When she awoke, she'd succumbed to a driving compulsion to take another shower. She'd scrubbed her skin until she was pink all over. It had helped a little. But not enough.

She lifted aside the drapes to gaze out at a sunset over Havana. Something seemed wrong with the daylight, all cheerful and normal out there. Didn't Mother Nature know she'd killed a man? It was still supposed to be dark outside, grim and black like her soul. As homeward-bound cars crowded the roads and pedestrians hurried to finish their daily business, none of them had any idea that last night she'd become a murderer.

The water cut off in the bathroom behind her. Mitch was in the shower now, although she highly doubted he was scrubbing his skin until it burned, trying to remove the indelible stains of death. The bathroom door opened on a rush of warm, humid air.

"Hungry?" Mitch murmured from close behind her.

"No. Thanks."

"You have to eat sometime. You need to keep your strength up."

"I don't think I could keep anything down right now."

She felt his sigh as much as heard it. "Getting over your first kill is always hard." He paused, as if searching for words. "I'm no expert at teaching anyone how to deal with it. You just sort of do."

She glanced over her shoulder at him, surprised. "Your first kill gave you trouble?"

He shrugged. "My first one was a buddy kill, so it wasn't nearly as…traumatic as yours."

"What's a buddy kill?"

"Two snipers shoot at the same target, a rookie and an experienced sniper. You both fire at the exact same instant, and that way you're not sure if your bullet or the other guy's killed the target. Makes it a little easier to wrap your brain around."

A fine shiver passed over her. "There's no doubt who blew that poor man's face off last night."

Mitch was beside her in an instant. "He wasn't a poor man, Kinsey. He was a hardened criminal. He worked for a cold-blooded killer and was no doubt a cold-blooded killer himself. You can be sure he was prepared to blow your face off without a second thought had he pulled the trigger just a little bit sooner than you."

Nausea roiled in her stomach. She hadn't even begun to deal with the fact that she'd nearly died, herself, yet. One trauma at a time.

She watched the beach far below, while Mitch stared silently out the window beside her. Eventually, he muttered. "I want to make it better, but I don't know how to comfort you."

She looked over at him in surprise. Mitch Perovski was expressing uncertainty about anything? Wow. He must be really rattled. His troubled gaze met hers for a moment and then slid away.

She replied, "It's not that hard. You put your arms around me and tell me it's going to be all right. And then I cry a little and you wipe away my tears."

He lifted the heavy curtain out of her hand and let it fall closed. The room plunged into nightlike darkness. His voice came out of the gloom. "How did that go again?"

"Arms. Around me."

His big form loomed close. Mitch's familiar hands slid around her waist, his strong, impossibly gentle embrace drawing her close and wrapping her in warmth. "Arms, check."

She smiled against his chest. "Now tell me it'll be okay."

"It'll be okay." Then he ad libbed, "I promise. It just takes a little time and distance." A pause. "How was that?"

Her smile widened. "That was fine."

"Now you're supposed to cry a little."

Her smile got even bigger. "Not happening right now."

He drew back to peer down at her. "Do you need me to make you cry?"

"No, that's okay. But thank you for offering."

They leaned into each other for several minutes in silence, resting in each other's company. Finally, she roused herself enough to murmur, "What's next for us?"

"Dunno. I'm not real experienced at this comforting stuff. I think I'm supposed to wipe away your tears once you have some for me to wipe."

"No, I mean what's next in the mission?"

"Oh." A pause. It stretched out until she wasn't entirely sure he was going to answer her. But then he said, "One of the men last night gave me an address before I...he...expired. Tonight, I'll go check it out."

"How do you know it's a real address and not a trap?"

A faint shrug beneath her cheek. "I don't. Only way to find out is to go see."

"I'm coming with you," she announced.

"Oh, no you're not," he retorted instantly.

"Oh, yes I am."

He leaned back a lot now, almost to the end of his reach. "This is not open to discussion. Last night was way too damned close a call. I'm not putting you in harm's way again like that."

"I put myself in harm's way, thank you very much. I'm the one who came after you out in the sand."

"And I'm not taking a chance on you pulling a foolish stunt like that again."

Indignation flared in her gut. She didn't stop to question whether or not it was the right reaction or too much reaction. "Hey. I saved your neck out there. Had I not warned you about those extra guys, who knows what would have happened?"

Mitch released her. Spun away. Paced the room once and came to a stop in front of her. "You were lucky. Plain and simple. It was sheer, dumb luck that you weren't killed out there."

She flared up. "Shooting that guy had nothing to do with luck! Who ran around and got those other guns and gave them to you? And who kept up with you up and down all those blasted sand dunes when I was so tired I wanted to sit down and die? None of that was luck."

"You don't know the first thing about field operations. You don't know how to do surveillance, how to tail someone, how to send or receive dead drops, how to work with a black ops team—"

She interrupted. "You and I made a pretty good team last night."

"We shot like crazy and hoped to hit them before they shot us. That's not teamwork. That's desperation."

She paced in irritation. "Why are you being like this? All that stuff you just listed off can be learned. The main thing is I didn't panic under fire and I kept moving. I might not have saved the day, but I also wasn't dead weight." She stopped prowling to glare at him. "I think you don't want me out in the field at all."

"Damned straight I don't want you out there."

She inhaled sharply. Had she misjudged him? Was he that big a chauvinist? He did say to Jennifer Blackfoot that he didn't like working with women. Her eyes narrowed. "Well, like it or not, you're stuck with me, so you might as well get used to it."

"As soon as I get rid of Camarillo, I'm getting rid of you. I'm sending you back to that catamaran and you're sailing out of here."

"What if I don't want to go? What if I want to see this operation through? I've already been seen around town. Won't it raise suspicion if suddenly you start hitting the dance clubs without me? Face it, Mitch. You need me. I'm your cover, and I'm a darned good one."

His gaze was dark and angry. He clearly did not like being maneuvered like this. But that was just tough. She was fighting for her future here. For her very identity as a useful, intelligent member of society. She was done hanging around the margins of life, pretty but useless, like…like…draperies!

She gritted her teeth and said as calmly as she could, "I killed a man for you. I've *earned* the right to be out there."

Their turbulent gazes locked, waging a silent struggle of wills. His was formidable, but she'd grown up with a dynamic and forceful politician for a father. She refused to back down. Finally, Mitch moved forward as fast as a striking snake and swept her up into his arms. His mouth swooped down upon hers, invading.

Like that wasn't a transparent tactic! But then his mouth moved against hers, mirroring the way his body moved sinuously, drawing her higher and closer into him, and her train of thought spun away like so much chaff on the wind. One of his big hands slid under her heavy, damp hair, cupping the back of her head.

"This isn't going to work," she grumbled against his lips. "You're not distracting me. I am staying with you."

She felt a tug at her waist and gasped as cool air wafted against her skin. And then his hands were on her body, sliding across her heated flesh and down to the small of her back. His fingertips stroked the sensitive spot at the base of her spine and she nearly sobbed with pleasure at the sensations ripping through her.

Then her right shoulder was bare. Cool air blew across it, but in a moment was replaced by the fire of his lips against her skin, kissing hot and wet, nipping at her just hard enough to make her wriggle.

"Mmm. You taste like candy."

"You taste like darkness."

He murmured against the column of her neck, "What does that taste like?"

"Wood smoke. And good vodka. Cool and biting with a hint of fire beneath."

"Honey, there isn't anything cool about me right now."

She laughed. "I don't know. The way you swagger around with those pistols is pretty cool."

He crushed her against him, and all but inhaled her. A charge of energy built between them, crackling and snapping, biting everywhere they touched, sending need screaming all the way to her toes. "I don't swagger."

"Do, too."

"Do not."

She raked her fingernails lightly down the side of his neck to trail down the bulging muscles of his chest. Her fingers brushed one edge of the bandage on his shoulder, a reminder of the danger of his work. "Fine. You prowl, then."

"I can live with that."

"And they say women have egos." She started and gave a little cry of surprise when he bent down suddenly, whipping an arm behind her knees and sweeping her off her feet. He carried her easily across the room.

"You're not the kind of woman who likes a man with no ego. You want a strong man who knows exactly what and who he is."

Until two days ago, she'd have laughed at the very notion of being attracted to macho, alpha males. In her experience, they were a royal pain to deal with. Give her some nice, quiet, thoughtful fellow with brains and good prospects for a secure future. Mitch wasn't particularly nice. He was…hard. Nor was he particularly quiet or reflective. He was decisive. A man of action. He was frighteningly intelligent, though. And exceedingly good at what he did. She wasn't sure about his future prospects. Spies must have a relatively short life span. No security in that.

But then he laid her down on the bed and commenced ably stripping her out of her bathrobe and underwear, and all thoughts of his prospects evaporated. The air-conditioned air sent a shiver across her skin. Or maybe Mitch's molten gaze, raking down her body, and flaring with heat was doing that to her. Hard to tell.

He started at her belly button, plunging his tongue into that incredibly sensitive spot, sending her straight up off the mattress and into his mouth again. Who'd have guessed her navel was connected to her female parts like that? Bolts of pure lust streaked through her. He kissed outward in ever expanding circles, causing her to alternately contract her stomach muscles into knots of pleasure, then to stretch, catlike, under the ministrations of his talented mouth. If he was a panther, then she was his main course as he feasted upon her flesh. And she hadn't a bone left in her body to protest.

"I want you, Kinsey," he murmured.

She groaned in the back of her throat, shuddering in too much pleasure to form words just then.

"I need you," he whispered.

She arched up into him, crying out as his mouth closed on the most sensitive parts of her, sending a jolt of pure sex all the way to her fingertips, so intense it robbed her of thought, let alone speech.

"And that's why you have to stay safe. For me."

And then he was looming up over her, bracing on arms wreathed in bulging, corded muscle. She reached up, desperate for more of what he was doing to her, and looped her hands around his neck, pulling him down to her.

"I'm only going to say this one more time. Make love to me, Mitch. Now."

A smile of purely male satisfaction flitted across his features, and then his gaze locked with hers. Went dead serious. Pierced straight into her soul. "Are you sure? There's no going back."

"Yes, I'm sure!" She'd never been more sure of anything in her life. Wave after wave of pounding need throbbed through her, carrying her out to sea like so much flotsam on the riptide of Mitch's mouth and hands and body upon hers.

And then the darkness descended upon her. Mitch's big body was against her and on her and in her, a stretching fullness that set her on fire, writhing upon a sword of desire that cut all the way through her, leaving no part of her whole. She flung herself against the muscular darkness that was Mitch, reveling in the strength that pinned her easily, enforcing his will upon her. And that will was pleasure. Intense, searing pleasure that tore cries from her throat and made her limbs weak and left her wanting more, and yet more, of him.

"Sing for me, Kinsey," he growled.

And sing she did. Sound started at the back of her throat and shuddered all the way down her body, until it was a keening, wordless moan of release that said everything that needed to be said. White light exploded behind her eyelids and a curtain of blackness fell over her mind in which nothing remained but exquisite, perfect sensation. And then the moment exploded in a shower of sparks that zipped through her and over her and around her. Death and rebirth. All in a single, infinite moment out of time.

She felt the explosion envelop Mitch, too, as his body shuddered and bucked against hers. He gave a hoarse shout of pleasure, the triumphant mating roar of the panther, king of his domain, and yet consumed by it.

They collapsed together, the velvety darkness wrapping around them gently. Slowly, Kinsey regained awareness of her surroundings, of Mitch's world—this place of primal instinct, of survival, of sex, of man and woman. It was all very simple, really.

He rolled to his back, gathering her against his side. Her arm fell across the slabbed muscles of his stomach, and yet again, she registered his outstanding physical condition. This was a man who would always keep moving. He would never be satisfied to sit around thinking about what needed to be done. He was the kind of man who would go do it. The kind of man a girl could put her trust in. He'd take care of her. Keep her safe. Provide for her. Love her unswervingly for all his days. Give her his complete loyalty until his dying breath. Mitch was the kind of man she could very easily love back—with the same intensity he'd love her.

"I'm not leaving you, Mitch."

"You don't have any choice in the matter. I've already told you I'll walk away. I wasn't kidding."

She pushed up onto her forearm on his chest and stared down at him in shock. "After what we just shared, you can still say that?"

She'd never noticed before how cold a metal gold could be. But it glittered out of his gaze harder and colder than any steel. *This* was what he'd been talking about when he'd warned her off him. He'd been right. She'd had no idea what he'd been talking about when he said he'd get inside her head, but he would still leave her. Oh, God.

"But I felt…I thought…" She couldn't finish the sentence. Had she really been that wrong about what they'd just shared? Was she that big a fool? Or—aloud, she asked, "Are you really that big a bastard?"

He looked her dead in the eye. "I *will* walk away from you. I promise you that."

Chapter 11

Mitch stared up miserably at the ceiling, cursing himself in every language he knew, as Kinsey climbed out of bed in silence and went into the bathroom. He *hated* doing that to her. And yet, he had no choice. No choice at all. He had to protect her. He cared for her too much not to. Making love with her had been a revelation. A light in the darkness, a moment of such perfection that he almost didn't dare to breathe, lest it disappear, with the one woman he'd searched for his whole life.

And he'd just broken her heart. Irrevocably made her hate him. Irretrievably ruined any chance they had for a future together. He sat up, swung his feet to the floor and hung his head. He swore luridly. His job sucked. His life sucked. *He* sucked.

He should walk away from it all. Grab Kinsey, head

for some deserted island on the other side of the world, and chuck the whole shooting match. Except he knew darn good and well that wouldn't slow down Camarillo or a slew of other men like him. A guy didn't work in this business for decades and not amass a lifetime supply of enemies. There were certain very careful protocols an operator must adhere to if he wanted to walk away from the business and live. And grabbing the girl and splitting was not part of that protocol. He swore some more.

No light seeped around the edges of the heavy curtains. Night had fallen while they were making love. Time for him to go to work. To become the only kind of man he knew how to be.

He stood up, suddenly feeling old. Tired. Sore. Or maybe that was just heartsore. Either way, his gut felt full of lead. He rummaged in his luggage and threw on some clothes.

He strapped a knife to his left calf, an ankle holster to his right leg. He shrugged into his double shoulder holster. By rote, he checked each weapon. Safety on. Fully loaded. A round chambered. Safety off. A throwing knife in the pocket at the back of his neck. Brass knuckles in the slot behind his front pocket, ammo clips in the rows of narrow slots along the back of his slacks, underneath his belt with its custom-designed garrote inside. Methodically, he armed himself with the tools of his trade, cursing every radio, every high-tech gadget, every lethal reminder of why he could never have Kinsey Hollingsworth for himself.

No woman in her right mind would cuddle up to a guy loaded down like a one-man army. A killing machine. He had to keep Kinsey safe. No matter what the cost. At *all* costs.

Janine had taught him well. The only way for a guy in his line of work to stay sane was not to love anything or anyone. He made a practice of maintaining no personal possessions of any value to him. No pictures, no memorabilia, no keepsakes with sentimental value. Nothing he'd feel bad about losing. He didn't get attached to his car, his guns, not even his music collection or books. All were expendable and replaceable. But he'd finally found the one thing—the one person— who was not expendable. And if he couldn't have her, he was damn well going to see to it she was safe.

With that grim resolve firmly in mind, he hefted his duffel bag and took one last look around the hotel room. No signs left behind to hint to Kinsey where he'd gone. He would walk out of here and not look back. That was the rule. He always walked away.

Except, of course, Kinsey had already broken all his rules, showing them up for the sham they'd really been. He had no illusions about leaving her behind. It would be neither easy nor clean. He'd given her a piece of himself today—a big, fat slice of his heart. And he would never get it back. Ah well, he hoped she had fun stomping all over it. He deserved anything she thought or said of him in the days to come. Worse, probably.

The doorknob turned under his hand. He muttered, "Goodbye Kinsey Hollingsworth. It was a pleasure knowing you."

Kinsey sat on the edge of the tub and listened to him go. She started when his quiet voice drifted through the flimsy bathroom door to her. *It was a pleasure…* He was leaving for good! She leaped up and ran out into the room.

All signs of him had disappeared. It was as if he'd never been here. His black duffel bag was gone, the clutter of weapons and wires and gadgets on the coffee table, all of it. Gone. She jumped to the door, and tore it open. She poked her head out into the hallway. No sign of him. She started to dart toward the elevators, then remembered she was buck naked. She couldn't run after him.

She raced back into the room and threw on clothes, grabbed her purse, and sprinted for the door. He wasn't getting away from her that easily. Whether she was going to kiss him or kill him when she caught up with him, she wasn't sure. She'd figure it out when the time came. But he wasn't getting away with this lame escape. She deserved better than that, and he was a better man than that—whether he was ready to admit it or not. He was going after Camarillo. And by golly she wasn't letting him do that alone.

She ran to the front doors of the hotel and collected herself enough not to burst out into the street like a panicked amateur. She looked both ways and spotted the black cruiser just pulling out of the hotel's parking lot. She stepped outside and opened the back door of a taxi sitting at the curb. Thankfully, her Spanish was adequate to convey to the driver that she'd like to follow that black sedan, but not too close. The driver threw her a sympathetic look and did as she asked.

As Mitch wound his way into a frankly dangerous looking part of town, the driver asked her if she wanted him to continue following the *señor.* She wasn't crazy about being out here by herself like this, and under normal circumstances, she'd tell the driver to take her back to the hotel. But these were not normal circumstances. And as distasteful as the thought of using it might be, she still had one gun in her purse.

Mitch's car pulled over at a curb and parked. Ducking into the shadows in the backseat of the cab, she had the driver continue on past. "Turn right up ahead," she directed.

The cabbie complied. There was an awkward moment when she realized she only had American greenbacks in her wallet, but the cabbie was eager to take them. With a warm thanks for his help, she paid him and sent him on his way. Time to go find her man.

She eased forward and peered around the corner. No sign of Mitch. Damn. She hadn't lost him already, had she? She moved forward cautiously. The street was dark, and the few people loitering in sight could be described as unsavory at best. So. This was Mitch's world, was it? She took a deep breath and concentrated on blending in. On breathing normally. On spotting her quarry.

There was no sign of Mitch anywhere. He'd disappeared. And none of the establishments along the sidewalk looked like the kind she could safely pop into for a minute to see if he was there. In desperation, she stopped to ask a middle-aged man minus most of his teeth and in need of a shave if he'd seen the man get out of that black car over there. The guy peered at her like she was a little green man from Mars gibbering some alien tongue. Hey. Her Spanish wasn't that bad. She pulled out a five-dollar bill and tried again.

Yup, cold hard cash was the universal translator. The fellow pointed at what looked like a bar.

Kinsey winced. She knew full well if she went inside, she'd get hit on by every unattached guy in the place. No way would she be able to hide from Mitch if he were in there. She considered her options. On a hunch, she moved over to his sedan and tried the doors. Bingo. The driver's side door was unlocked. He probably did that so he could make a quick getaway if need be.

She opened the door quickly. Not surprisingly, the overhead bulb didn't go on. Mitch had no doubt removed it. She crawled into the backseat and rummaged in Mitch's duffel bag, coming up with one of his black turtlenecks. She pulled it on over her light-colored shirt. She found a black T-shirt next and tore it into a rough headscarf. She wrapped it over her dark hair and left an end trailing down to pull over her face when the time came. It was the best she could do for camouflage. Then, she wriggled down onto the floor—thank goodness these old cars had tons of legroom—and pulled the duffel bag forward to hang off the edge of the seat so it mostly covered her hiding place.

And then she waited. It was hot and stuffy in the car, and before long, her cramped position became unbearably uncomfortable. She sat up twice, stretching out kinked muscles and cracking open one of the rear doors for a few seconds to let in some fresh air. What in the world was Mitch doing in there? He said he was going to pay Camarillo a visit tonight. And he never mixed booze and guns, so he wasn't likely drinking. Maybe working a contact? Finding out more about Camarillo's place before he barged in on the killer?

She passed the time thinking about making love with Mitch. And she arrived at several conclusions. First, she hadn't imagined the intense emotional connection between the two of them. Second, Mitch had felt it, too. Third, he might have walked away from her like he said he was going to, but he wasn't happy about it. And that meant there was still hope for them.

Maybe she was just being pitifully clingy or overly needy, but she wasn't ready to give up on him. If that made her a stalker, so be it. He was going to have to look her in the eye and tell her he wanted nothing more to do with her, that making love with her had meant nothing to him, before she was walking away from him—or letting him walk away from her.

Nearly two hours had passed when her senses abruptly went on full alert. Someone was coming. She covered her face with the dark cloth and lay perfectly still. The driver's door opened and someone got into the front seat. The engine started and the car pulled away from the curb. Assuming that was Mitch driving, she'd done it! He hadn't discovered her!

She had no idea that riding on the floor of a car was so bloody uncomfortable. She braced herself as best she could as the vehicle banged over the old roads of Cuba. Where was he going? The city noises outside faded, and the ride became even worse. Finally, it sounded like gravel began to spit out from under the tires. A dirt road, maybe?

The engine cut off. The car coasted to a stop. Silence enveloped the vehicle. Kinsey waited breathlessly. What was he waiting for? Finally, the front door opened and a cacophony of night sounds burst into the car. The door slammed shut. Kinsey gave him a few seconds, then sat up painfully and peered out over the rim of a window. His dark shape was just disappearing into the bushes. Quickly, she scrambled to her feet and slipped out the back door. Scared to death, she crept into the jungle after him.

Thankfully, his passing left a faint trail of crushed weeds and an absence of dew upon the dense foliage. She was able to move with relative ease along the pseudo-trail he blazed through the jungle. How far ahead of her he was, she had no idea. She did know it would be a bad thing to surprise him from behind. She'd seen his reflexes in action, and he'd shoot her before he ever saw her face if she wasn't careful.

The ground began to rise and instinct made her slow down. She dropped to her knees and traveled the last few yards up the slope on her hands and knees. She sincerely hoped there were no poisonous snakes or scorpions or worse out here, because she couldn't see a blessed thing. A glow illuminated the other side of the hill. On her belly, she eased forward a few more feet. And stared at the compound sprawling before her. It was more than a villa. It was a whole collection of buildings behind a heavy fence and lit with spotlights.

The lights threw a series of dark shadows up the hillside toward her. Searching carefully from her vantage point, she picked out a dark form supine on the ground. Was that Mitch? She watched it for several minutes. And then, very slowly, the shadow moved. She'd know that sinuous grace anywhere. After all, she'd held all that sleek power in her arms. Oh, yes. That was Mitch.

He inched forward, moving from one shadow to the

next, pausing frequently. If he'd had a tail, its tip would have twitched like a panther's. Mitch was hunting tonight.

She watched him for nearly a half hour, easing his way closer and closer to the buildings. At one point, she thought she saw him slowly lift a pair of binoculars to his eyes. What did he see? Had he spotted Camarillo?

She wouldn't have believed it possible two days ago, but she desperately hoped Mitch found the guy and killed him. She was ready to get on with her relationship with Mitch. Until the threat of Camarillo was removed, it would hang between them, a piece of unfinished business that would prevent either of them from moving on with their lives.

Mitch moved again, edging past the last of the boulders dotting the hillside. All that was left between him and the fence was a stretch of long grass, its seed heads nodding in a gentle whiff of night air. The mosquitoes were ferocious, and Kinsey couldn't stand them any longer. She slid back a few feet and dug in her purse for the tiny bottle of concentrated bug spray Jennifer Blackfoot had told her to put in her bag back at the ops center. God bless Jennifer.

Quickly, Kinsey rubbed the oily stuff on her skin. A faint musty odor rose from it. She pocketed the bottle and made her way back to the crest of the hill. Mitch had disappeared into the grass somewhere. She waited patiently, her gaze on the fence he would eventually have to get past. He would probably head for that shadowed area where a clump of palmettos butted up against the fence from the inside. She guessed it would take him fifteen minutes to make his way over there.

She studied the grass carefully, and although she

spotted a number of suspicious waves of seed heads over the open stretch that didn't look like the breeze blowing, she couldn't spot Mitch.

His fifteen minutes was nearly up when an explosion of motion below caused her to jolt violently. What the—

No less than ten black-clad forms erupted up out of the grass, shouting. They bore weapons, and all of them were pointed at roughly the patch of grass in front of the palmettos. A second violent movement made her jump, this time the familiar silhouette of Mitch springing up out of the grass and sprinting back toward her position. More shouting and the other men leaped forward.

Mitch never had a chance. The men tackled him and bodily subdued him. He put up a heck of a fight and even with ten men on top of him, gave them a hard time. Finally, she saw the butt of a rifle rise up in the air and fall. She all but came over the hill in her horror. The heaving pile of men went still.

It was a trap! *And Mitch had walked right into it.* She felt hot all over. Sick to her stomach. She had to *do* something. But what? She couldn't take out that many men by herself even if she knew what to do! The group lifted Mitch's limp form and four men staggered forward under his weight. They moved along the fence, but made no effort to go inside the compound, even bypassing a gate.

Frantic to do something, she followed along the ridge, paralleling the men, peeking over the top of it every few yards to check on the men's progress. Her ridge disappeared into trees, and she struggled to move through them quietly, skirting the edge of the jungle, in the foliage deeply enough to avoid being seen, but close enough to keep visual contact with Mitch. The men carried him around the perimeter of the compound and peeled off through the trees. The going got thicker here and she lost sight of them. In desperation, she battled her way closer to where she'd last seen them. A trail, no doubt trampled by the large group in front of her, unfolded. She raced along it as quietly as she could. She couldn't lose Mitch!

Startled, she heard an engine rev in front of her. She darted forward and emerged at the edge of a clearing in time to see two sets of taillights disappear down the road in front of her. Her stomach dropped sickly. She'd lost him. She raced in the opposite direction, praying this was the same road on which Mitch had parked his car.

Panic tightened her chest and made her so jittery she could hardly stay on her feet. Gasping for air she sprinted down the road, searching frantically for the car. It had been half hidden in a clump of bushes, and its black color would further camouflage it. She almost ran past it, but a glimmer of glass finally caught her attention.

She jumped in the front seat. No keys. She hunted furiously in the map pockets and under floormats. *C'mon, Mitch. Where'd you hide the key?* There was no sign of it. Frustrated and close to tears, she slumped in the seat. Now what?

She twisted to reach into the back seat for Mitch's duffel bag. She lifted the heavy bag into the front seat beside her and commenced rifling through it. There had to be something useful in here. The seconds were ticking away and those cars were getting farther and farther away from her.

She dug past clothes and tools and ammunition desperately. Aha. A hybrid radio-telephone looking thing. She yanked it out. She examined the switches and pressed what looked like a power button. The face glowed faintly. She pressed it to her ear. Static. It had a keypad that looked like telephone numbers. Who to call? There was no 911 in Cuba for illegal spies in need of rescue.

The Bat Cave. If she could get hold of Mitch's headquarters, maybe they could help. A phone number for them…she wracked her brains, but couldn't for the life of her remember the phone number on Jennifer Blackfoot's desk phone.

She examined the phone and started pressing random buttons. A menu popped up on the screen. She scrolled down through a bunch of unhelpful sounding choices. How she ended up at a phone book of stored numbers, she wasn't quite sure. But she thanked her lucky star and thumbed through the entries. They were all seemingly random sequences of letters and numbers. Codes, probably.

Then one caught her attention. ICE11.

She'd heard a bit on the news not long ago about programming an emergency contact phone number into your cell phone and labeling it I-C-E, which stood for In Case of Emergency. Apparently EMTs and police often found the cell phones of victims at accident and crime scenes but then had no idea who, out of a list of stored phone numbers, to call to notify a friend or family member. But ICE numbers solved that problem.

What the heck. The worst she could do was end up waking up some general or foreign spy. She hit the auto dial button for ICE 11.

It only rang once. A male voice bit out, "Go."

"Uhh, who is this?" she asked.

"Who the hell is this?" the male voice exclaimed.

"I can't tell you. This is an emergency, though. Who am I speaking to?"

"This is a government phone number...Kinsey? Is that you?"

She started. "Yes, it's me. Who is this?"

"Brady Hathaway. What are you doing on this line?"

Thank God. The Bat Cave. Relief nearly made her throw up. She spoke all in a rush. "Mitch has been kidnapped. I was following him, but he didn't know. And I saw him get jumped by about ten guys. They knocked him out and carried him to the road, but I lost sight of them. They threw him in a car and drove away. I'm in Mitch's car now but I can't find a key and it won't start and I don't know what to do—"

"Slow down, there, Kinsey. Take a deep breath. You did the right thing to call us. We've got all kinds of resources to help Mitch. There's no need to panic, okay?"

Hathaway's voice was calm and completely unruffled. He didn't seem the slightest bit concerned about Mitch's predicament. She did as he suggested and took several slow, deep breaths.

"I'm going to go off the horn for a couple minutes. I'm passing you to a guy named John Hollister. He's going to keep talking to you while I do a few things to help Mitch. Okay?"

"Okay."

Another man came on the line. He also had a soothing voice that conveyed that everything was under control. He gently questioned her, talking her through all the details of the evening up till this point. At the end of her recitation, he commented, "You've done very well, Kinsey. Your quick thinking may very well save Mitch's life."

She lurched. She'd almost forgotten in these guys' calmness that Mitch was in serious trouble.

Then Hollister surprised her by saying, "I'm going to talk you through how to hot-wire a car. Do you think you're up to it?"

She blinked, startled. "I guess so."

"You said you had Mitch's bag of tools, yes?"

"Yes."

"Reach inside and look for a pair of wire cutters and a pair of pliers. Do you know what both of those look like?"

She laughed. "Shockingly enough, I do know what those look like. And believe me, not too many of the women I know do."

She heard the smile in Hollister's voice. "You're going to do just fine, Kinsey. Now. You may need to open the car door and kneel on the ground to do this, but look on the bottom side of the steering column and find a screw. It'll be recessed in a little tube and may be hard to see in the dark...."

It took nearly a half hour, and there was a delay while someone was found who knew the wiring of a vintage 1950s automobile ignition system, but eventually, the sedan's engine roared to life.

Hollister congratulated her on hot-wiring her first car and passed her back to Brady Hathaway.

"Hi Kinsey, it's me again, Brady."

"Hey."

"Okay. I've got a team of SEALs en route to your

area. They'll be on the ground in six hours. It may take them a few more hours to join you. They'll be equipped and ready to rescue Mitch."

She let out a long breath of relief.

"We're going to give you directions, and you're going to drive to Havana and go to the American Embassy. We'll call them and they'll be waiting for you."

"No!"

"Kinsey—"

"Brady. I'm not arguing with you about this." She put the car in gear and eased it forward, accelerating when she reached the road. "I'm following Mitch."

"Kinsey, Camarillo is a big-time assassin, and you're an amateur. Your father's a congressman, for God's sake."

"And I'll raise heck through him if you don't help me find Mitch," she hesitated.

"Not a chance," Brady retorted flatly.

"Let's review. I'm in Cuba, I'm driving along a road and may stumble into Camarillo's men all by myself. I'm a hysterical female…oh, and I have a gun. I'm doing this whether you help me or not. Now, are you going to sit back and let the congressman's daughter get herself killed, or are you going to do your best to help her and keep her alive?"

A long, frustrated silence was her only reply.

Finally, Brady growled, "Fine. Have it your way. But let the record show I'm doing this under duress."

"So noted," Kinsey replied dryly.

"If we let you help us find Mitch and give us eyes-on intelligence about where he is, will you *promise* not to do anything stupid and to wait for our SEAL team to extract him?"

"If it'll help Mitch, I promise."

A heavy sigh. "Pull out onto the road and proceed in the direction you're currently headed. I've got your car on the satellite."

"You mean you're looking at me right now?" she asked in surprise.

"If you stuck your arm out the window and waved at me, I'd see it," Hathaway replied grimly.

Wow. She'd heard the U.S. had some crazy powerful satellites, but knowing that cameras were peering down at her from space right now was kind of creepy.

Hathaway continued, "You'll go straight ahead for about ten miles. Take a look at your odometer, okay?"

"It says 599,221."

"Damn, they get a lot out of those cars," Hathaway muttered. "I gotta get me a Cuban mechanic."

"How old is this car, anyway?" she asked to distract herself as she drove.

"Probably pushing sixty years old. At the next intersection, you're going to turn right. It'll be a paved road. There may be a stop sign…I can't make it out in the dark."

Definitely creepy. She slowed down as what looked like a yield sign loomed in her headlights. For the next hour, she followed Hathaway's instructions and actually found herself unwinding a little from her earlier panic. It felt good to be doing something, not just sitting around worrying about Mitch.

Then Hathaway said, "Slow down. Turn off your headlights if you can."

"I can." She did as he asked, her pulse spiking hard.

"Stop wherever you can. If the ground looks solid, pull completely off the road and get behind some cover. Let me know when you've done that."

She crawled along in the dark, peering at the shadows until she found a thick clump of plants similar to the one Mitch had parked behind earlier. She maneuvered the cumbersome car behind the bushes. "Okay, done."

"Carefully pull apart the white wire and the blue wire without touching the exposed copper and bend them back so they won't touch. The engine should stop."

"Done."

"Now, in Mitch's bag, I need you to look for a few things."

Once Hathaway had armed her with a big pair of field glasses, night-vision goggles, an earbud for the satellite phone and a really big gun, he directed her to get out of the car. Leaving the door unlocked, she stepped out into the night. Once more, she was entering Mitch's dark, shadow world, and once more, she felt completely unequal to the task. But he was out here somewhere and in grave danger. She *had* to help him.

"How do you hear me?" Hathaway murmured into her earpiece.

"Fine," she murmured back.

"When you get close to the target location, you can respond to me by clicking that long black button on the side of the phone. One click means no and two clicks means yes. Got it?"

She double-clicked in response.

"Good girl. Okay, you're going on a little hike. I

can't see you through the canopy of trees, but your phone has a GPS locator in it. You'll have to find your own way through the jungle and around any obstacles you run into. I'll give you course corrections to the left or right, but do what you have to in order to keep moving forward. Whatever you do, don't grab at any sticks or vines for balance. They could be a snake. And don't walk between any trees that seem to have a wide open space between them without clearing the space first with a long stick. Spiders like to make webs between trees."

"You sure know how to give a girl warm fuzzies."

"You're doing great. Just hang in there with me."

"Here goes nothing," she mumbled, and plunged into the wall of black-green before her.

The trek was a nightmare. Sharp leaves slashed at her arms like swords. Fallen trees tripped her, and vines and weeds clutched at her ankles. Were it not for Brady's constant course corrections, she'd have become hopelessly lost in the thick tangle of undergrowth. Sometimes the jungle pressed in on her so thickly she feared she couldn't move any of her limbs and was completely trapped. Only worry for what was happening to Mitch drove her to fight on, to wrestle against the living breathing beast that had swallowed her whole.

When an impossibly thick vine slithered up into the trees right in front of her, she completely lost her composure. That snake had been as big around as her arm and easily ten feet long.

"Not to worry," Hathaway soothed as she hyperventilated in his ear. "That was a tree boa. They're more afraid of you than you are of them."

He allowed her a few minutes to rest and collect herself, and then he urged her onward again. "Not much further to go. Mitch's signal is located under tree cover, so I can't tell you what you're walking into."

"Don't you guys have infrared cameras or something where you can see heat signatures through walls?"

"Been watching cable TV, huh?" he commented. "Yeah, we do. But for some reason we're not painting any signatures. They're probably inside some sort of metal structure that reflects the signal, or maybe underground. That's what we need you to tell us."

She gathered her remaining energy and slogged on. *I'm coming Mitch. Just hang on.* As the minutes ticked past, she began to get a sick feeling in the pit of her stomach. It expanded into a cramplike feeling not centered in any one place. Something bad was happening to Mitch. She felt his pain as if it were her own. She tried to ignore the sensation, to reason with herself that it was just her frazzled nerves and overactive imagination, but the feeling kept getting stronger and stronger. The endless, throbbing ache would not be ignored.

"Something bad's happening to Mitch," she announced to Hathaway.

He replied sharply, "Can you hear him?"

"No. I can feel him." She added hastily, "I'm not just being a hysterical female here. I have this unshakable feeling in my gut that he's in pain."

"I believe you," Hathaway replied grimly. "I learned a long time ago to pay attention to gut feelings like yours. You've got about two hundred yards to go."

Two hundred steps. She counted them off in her head, thanking the stars when she reached open patches and could go ten or twelve steps unimpeded, and cursing the stars when she had to struggle forward a few inches at a time. And still the feeling in her gut grew. It was a sharp pain now.

"Twenty yards. Slow down and don't make any more verbal responses to me. Clicks only. Take a good look around, then retreat thirty yards or so into the jungle and give me a call to report what you see."

She double-clicked her understanding. Those last few yards were torture. An urge to bolt forward, to run screaming into the middle of whatever was going on, to find Mitch and rescue him, to stop the knifelike ghost pains shooting through her body, nearly overwhelmed her.

She eased forward, testing each step before she put her foot down. And then a small glade became visible through the trees. She eased forward, one foot at a time, sticking to the deepest shadows. A few minutes ago, they'd been frightening, but now those shadows were her friend, embracing her in their inky camouflage, bringing her closer to the man she craved.

A one-story, galvanized metal building with rust stains streaming down its sides stretched before her. Two men armed with rifles of some kind lounged at one end of it. The structure had no windows that she could see. She eased off to her left, circling the back of the building. The end opposite the guards had a small window up high, above a banged-up looking air-conditioner unit. Some sort of vent opened up beside it at ground level, covered with a screen. It looked like a fan from inside the building blew through the lower opening. The far side of the building yielded no more windows.

She crouched on her heels and tried to figure out what else Hathaway and his SEALs would need to know to attack this place. She moved closer to the front and the guards. Two vans stood out front. Probably the same vehicles she'd seen pulling away from the site of Mitch's kidnapping. Which meant around eight more men must be inside the building. She noted electric lines running overhead into the structure, a glow of light coming from the closed front door. It looked like the place had a concrete foundation that probably formed a floor. A few of the galvanized panels on this side of the building looked loose along the bottom.

And it was deathly quiet. All the jungle creatures, even the insects, were silent. A heavy, expectant hush blanketed the whole place.

And then a hoarse scream pierced the night. It tore through her like no sound she'd ever heard before. There was a loud crackle of noise, like lightning frying a bug, and the strip of light under the door flickered. Another hoarse shout of agony.

Oh. My. God.

Mitch.

Chapter 12

Mitch sagged against the wet ropes binding him to the metal chair. These boys hadn't missed a trick. The only reason he wasn't dead right now was because of the building's inferior wiring. An air conditioner labored behind him, stealing most of the electricity, and the current left over was barely sufficient to light a few bulbs overhead. While it was excruciatingly painful, it wasn't anywhere close to lethal. Thank God his torturers wanted to be comfortable and run the A/C while he suffered.

He studied his captors from beneath swollen lids. The bastards were military. He was sure of it. He thought he'd glimpsed a couple uniforms in the scrum when they jumped him back at Camarillo's estate. The men standing in front of him now, arguing over how much more to torture him before they went to get something to eat, were lean. Fit. Short-haired. All below the age of forty. Nope. Not Camarillo's men. The Cuban assassin was in his sixties and tended to hang out with his childhood friends, whom he trusted.

Who then?

And then, he glimpsed a familiar insignia on the chest of the guy giving the orders. The Presidential Guard.

These were Zaragosa's men. The Cuban official had double-crossed him. Double-crossed the U.S. government. The Americans thought the guy was their loyal ally, but who knew what sort of misinformation he was feeding U.S. intelligence agencies? He *had* to get out of here and let someone know Zaragosa was unreliable!

If he was going to share what he knew, he was going to have to live long enough to get out of here. And at the moment, that prospect wasn't looking great.

He'd never dreamed Camarillo and Zaragosa might actually be in league. Hell, no one had. But now that he thought about it, he had to ask himself how Camarillo's men had known about the scheduled meeting with Zaragosa back in the Virgin Islands in time to show up early at the rendezvous point, lay an ambush, and nearly kill him. Damn. It had been right there in front of him the whole time.

And he'd been so besotted with lust for Kinsey he hadn't stopped long enough to think about it. To see the connection. She'd tried to tell him. She'd asked how Camarillo had found him, and he'd ignored her because she was an amateur. God, he'd nearly gotten her killed because he hadn't been paying attention to her brains instead of her body. Stupid. Very, very stupid of him. And now he was paying the price for it.

He should've left her a note. At least told her what he

was doing, if not where he was going tonight. But no. He'd been so focused on being noble, on walking away, on sacrificing his heart for her safety, that he'd neglected Spycraft 101—tell somebody where you're going, particularly when it involves engaging the bad guys.

Hell, he probably deserved this excruciating pain shooting through him like a thousand knives. He'd already gone through the mental exercise of separating himself from the agony, of compartmentalizing it in a walled-off corner of his mind. It took a certain amount of concentration to maintain the disconnect between himself and intense suffering, but he'd practiced the technique for years. It was manageable. And because his captors didn't know the technique, they projected themselves into his shoes and mistakenly assumed they were inflicting unbearable amounts of pain upon him. Throw in a few screams now and then to convince them they were right, and the situation was under control.

For the moment. Once they started trying to extract information from him that would change. Then they'd steadily up the pain factor until they broke down both him and his walls and forced him to talk. Although, so far they'd shown no inclination to interrogate him. Which lent even further credibility to the evidence that these were Zaragosa's men. They weren't here to find out who he was. They already knew.

One of the men stepped over to the crude rheostat sitting on the table against the far wall. Playtime with electricity again. *Damn that Benjamin Franklin.* Mitch closed his eyes. Retreated down the long corridor of his mind, far, far away from the room in which he'd closeted all sensation from his twitching, jerking, spasming body.

* * *

Nearly crying aloud in pain, Kinsey backed away into the jungle far enough so the guards couldn't possibly hear her and keyed her microphone. "Are you there?" she whispered.

"Go ahead," Hathaway replied immediately.

"He's in a building. And I think they're torturing him." Her voice caught on the word.

"Why do you think that?"

She took a steadying breath. She couldn't very well tell this man she was having sympathy pains. He'd think she was nuts. Instead, she replied, "I heard him yelling. It's terrible." She added in a rush, "You have to do something. Get him out of there!"

"We're on our way, Kinsey."

"When? When will you get here?"

"Soon."

"How soon?"

"Four, maybe five hours."

"He won't make it that long!"

A sigh. "Here's the thing. Mitch is a trained operative. That means a couple things. First, he can take a hell of a lot of pain without cracking. Second, he may be shouting in hopes of someone hearing him. He could be using the excuse of getting roughed up a little to make a lot of noise."

Kinsey frowned. That wasn't what the sharp tingling in her limbs was telling her. "I dunno...he sounded pretty awful. Like the noise was being ripped out of him."

"Trust me. He'll be okay. Now, I need you to tell me everything you saw."

Hathaway spent the next ten minutes picking details out of her she hadn't even registered seeing—insignia on uniforms, exterior building lighting, terrain features. She was actually impressed at everything she had seen.

"Now what?" she asked.

"Now you sit tight. I'm not kidding. Don't mess with this situation. You've done what you could. When the SEALs get there, they'll handle the situation."

He was right. But the wrenching cramps clenching her body in a vise of pain said otherwise. How long could Mitch suffer like this and live? Heck, how long could she take it?

Hathaway was talking again. "Hang out in the fringe of the jungle and keep an eye on things. If anything changes—more men come or some men leave, or you hear any gunshots, that sort of thing—back into the underbrush and give us a call. Okay?"

"Okay."

"You're doing great. Just stay calm and try not to worry too much. This will all work out."

Easy for him to say. He didn't have to listen to Mitch's suffering. To *feel* it.

She did as Hathaway said and quietly made her way back to the edge of the little glade. She found a good spot to lie down and peer under some sort of fern-ish plant at the guards still lounging out front.

A jolt of agony shot through her, and another scream rent the night. Oh, God. Mitch. Tears streamed down her face unchecked. She couldn't do this. She couldn't lie here and listen to him dying by inches. And yet…she had to. He might not know it, but he wasn't alone. She was with him, if not physically, in spirit. She reached out with her mind and heart, begging him to feel her presence, to know she cared for him and was here for him.

How long the torture went on, she didn't know. She was afraid to look at her watch and find out how long Mitch had endured whatever they were doing to him in there. It felt like days. Weeks. Forever. She might not actually be suffering the same intensity of pain he was, but her ghost pains and her mental suffering, knowing what he was going through, were almost more than she could bear. With each renewed wave of agony that washed over her, a little more of her control slipped away, a little more of her soul was stripped bare.

The social niceties of her upbringing ceased to matter. Her family's wealth and position and power couldn't help her or Mitch now. Her need to prove herself didn't matter anymore. Mitch's stubborn refusal to acknowledge what they had between them revealed itself for the sham it was. The two of them had played all kinds of games with each other, danced all around their attraction—and ultimately, their feelings—for one another. Mitch had even obeyed his stupid rule about always walking away.

But when all of that was burned away by the fiery pain of their mutual torture, only two things remained that mattered.

She and Mitch both had to live.

And she loved him.

The only remaining question was whether or not she'd ever get a chance to tell him that.

Eventually, there came a lull. Maybe Mitch passed out, or maybe his captors took a break. But either way the pain stopped. She was almost more startled by its absence than its presence. Somewhere in the past few hours, she'd forgotten what not-pain felt like. It was a shock to her now.

And somehow she knew to dread the return of pain even more after having been granted this brief reprieve.

She was right.

A jolt of fury shot through her without warning, arching her entire body into a bow of agony so intense she couldn't even breathe. It went on and on and on until she thought she might pass out. And then it subsided, only to return a few seconds later. Panic washed over her. It was too much. They were breaking him. Breaking her.

Mitch! She mentally screamed out for him.

Silence was her only reply.

She couldn't stand it anymore. She had to do something. They were ripping Mitch's guts out, and they were tearing hers out at the same time. Like it or not, she and Mitch shared some sort of invisible, but very real connection. His pain was hers, his panic hers. She knew without a shadow of a doubt that Mitch needed to get out of there, and soon. His urgency flowed through every pore of her being.

No way was Hathaway's SEAL team going to get here soon enough. Mitch's captors were all about causing him pain. This wasn't an interrogation he could draw out indefinitely while he eked out bits and pieces of information between rounds of torture. These men wanted to cause him suffering. And at some point they would tire of the game and put a gun to his head. How she knew all that, she couldn't say. But she knew it as certainly as she was lying here in the middle of the jungle.

She wriggled backward until she could safely stand up and backed away from the building. She keyed the microphone. "It's me again."

"Go ahead," Hathaway replied immediately.

"If I were going to go in there and rescue Mitch, how would you suggest I do it?"

"Don't even *think* about it," Hathaway growled. "You've got no training, no skills, no chance. If you go barging in there, you'll get Mitch killed. Do you understand me? Don't do anything."

She replied pleasantly, "If I hadn't grown up with a congressman who's used to getting his way for a father, that tone of voice might intimidate me, Commander."

Hathaway swore freely in her ear. He saw where this was going.

She continued, "But here's the deal. I'm standing here, a hundred feet from Mitch, and you're not. Neither he nor I can take anymore of this. I am going in there to get him out, and you're not stopping me. Now, are you going to help me figure out a way to do it that *will* succeed, or am I on my own?"

"Stand by. Give us a minute to toss around some ideas."

"All right."

"Promise?" he demanded.

"I will if you will," she retorted.

"We're going to come up with a plan for you to execute. I swear. Just sit tight for a couple minutes, okay?"

"Okay."

Probably five minutes passed. Mitch wasn't shouting right now. Either the bad guys were taking a break, or he'd passed out. She wasn't getting any gut feels at the moment that indicated which one was the case. But at least she wasn't experiencing any crippling pains spreading outward from her backbone to her fingertips and toes. For that, she was abjectly grateful.

Then Hathaway's voice startled her. Without preamble, he said, "Question. Are you willing to kill people or not?"

"Which one will give Mitch a better chance of walking out of there alive?"

He grunted. "The lethal option is by far the more effective way to go in this scenario."

She took a deep breath. She couldn't believe she was saying this, but faced with the alternative, it suddenly wasn't that awful a choice. "Then, I'm willing to kill. I've done it before. I'll do it again if I have to if that's what it takes to save Mitch."

"All right." In the background, she heard him say to someone, "She'll pull the trigger if it comes to it. Give me one more walk-through on Plan A." To her, he said, "Give me one more minute. And then we'll be ready to go."

Kinsey duly waited, and true to his word, Hathaway was back in a few moments. "Okay, Kinsey. Here's what we're going to do...."

Chapter 13

Time lost all meaning for Mitch. He measured it in minutes for a while, then in moments between waves of pain, and then in individual breaths. Apparently, his captors had decided to finish him off before they took off to get a bite to eat. Bastards.

He nurtured the spark of anger, blew gently on it with a pep talk to himself that he'd outlast these yahoos, piled the dry tinder of Kinsey's smile and his desperate need to get back to her on the tiny flame, and gradually, it caught. A fire grew in his belly that he fanned into a roaring flame of determination to survive. He was going to see Kinsey again. He was going to lie beside her and feel her arms around him, kiss her sweet lips, lose himself in the infinite warmth of her eyes. These petty little twerps weren't going to stand in his way. He'd outlast them no matter what they threw at him.

Maybe they sensed the change in him, the renewed strength, for they broke off electrocuting him abruptly, cursing. One of them swore for a while and declared himself hungry and tired of this crap.

Mitch watched his captors carefully from the swollen slits of his eyes. Were they tired enough of messing with him to kill him now, or would they cook up some new and improved way to make him suffer? He thought fast. If they made a move to off him, he'd have to talk fast to prevent it. He rehearsed what he was going to say to give them pause.

A murmured argument ensued across the room. The jerk in charge's hand came to rest on the pistol holster at his waist. Crap. They were leaning toward just offing him now. He sat up straight, ignoring the agonizing protest from his abused kidneys. He shifted his weight so his chair scraped the floor loudly. All eyes turned toward him. His chin went up.

"Is that the best you can do?" he commented casually in Spanish. It hurt his loosened front teeth to talk, but he endured the shouting nerves in his mouth. Pain, no matter how bad, was preferable to death.

The men's eyebrows shot up in surprise, then slammed together in fury.

So much for a midnight snack, boys.

Snarling, they advanced on him, all thoughts of finishing this off fast gone from their minds.

I win.

The first heavy fist landed on his upraised jaw. His head snapped back and white shards of pain exploded behind his eyes.

Sort of.

* * *

Kinsey lay on the ground behind a fallen log only twenty-five feet or so from the front door of the metal building. She couldn't believe Hathaway and company had actually let her move in this close to the soldiers lounging on the fenders of their vans. She could smell the smoke from their inferior cigarettes. Mitch was seriously going to owe her one when this was all over. She refused to consider the idea of failure. She *would* rescue Mitch and both of them would walk out of this in one piece.

Another groan issued from the building, this time genuine agony. Kinsey all but doubled over from the pain. Her face felt on fire, her ribs ached until she could hardly breathe, and every bone in her body screamed its suffering.

Hathaway's voice was emotionless in her ear. "Final target locked in. Fire on my command in three…two… one…bombs away."

Somewhere high overhead, a Predator unmanned aerial vehicle was loitering, looking down on this nightmare. And it had just launched its pair of onboard Hellfire missiles at the two vans directly in front of her. Hathaway had warned her it would be dangerous to be this close to the targets, but she didn't trust her marksmanship any farther away from the door than this.

Hathaway spoke sharply. "Get down flat behind cover. Eyes closed, hands over your ears. Contact in five…four…three…"

His voice was drowned out by a faint but distinct whistling noise that quickly built to a scream too loud even for her hands clapped over her ears to block.

And then the explosions detonated. Almost simultaneous, she barely distinguished the first from the second. The combined flash of light washed over her first, followed a millisecond later by a concussion of sound so loud it made her entire body hurt. The ground jumped beneath her and dirt and twigs and leaves showered down upon her.

"Direct hit, gentlemen. You're on, Kinsey."

Still so stunned by the explosion that she felt numb all over, she nonetheless poked her head up from behind the log. Two blazing hulls were all that was left of the vans. The two guards lounging against them had been vaporized. The front wall of the building was dented in, the door hanging askew in its frame. On cue, someone from inside leaped into the doorway. She took careful aim with the MP-4 submachine gun from Mitch's black duffel bag, and pulled the trigger. The weapon leaped in her hands and she fought to bring the muzzle back down into a firing position quickly.

She had no time to stop and think about having killed someone as the man lurched backward and fell, for another man appeared in the doorway. She pulled the trigger again. A secondary explosion rocked one of the burning van remains, and a third man staggered back into the building before she could get off a shot at him.

"Are they shooting back at you?" Hathaway bit out.

"No," she ventured to murmur into the radio. "Maybe they think the two guys I shot were hit by shrapnel. They're dragging them inside now."

"The explosions removed some of the canopy of tree cover. We have visual on part of the clearing now. Keep picking off guys in the doorway until they start shooting back. Then bug out."

"Got it," she replied grimly.

She felt nothing. So intensely focused was she on saving Mitch, she had no time for emotion. No time for horror. No time for moral self-recriminations. These guys were trying to kill Mitch, she was trying to kill them. The logic was simple. Clean. Straightforward.

Another man appeared in the doorway. She took aim and pulled the trigger. The side of his head exploded in a blossom of red. He spun, staggered outside against the wall, reached clumsily for the weapon at his hip. She pulled the trigger again, this time taking aim at the center of his chest.

He dropped to the ground.

She swung her sight back to the doorway. Two men came out this time, guns blazing. She dived down behind her log. They were firing wildly, although a few shots winged by overhead. Time to go. She crawled backward on her belly, getting covered in muck and slime as she dragged herself through a puddle.

"You're clear," Hathaway announced. "Get up and run."

She sprinted through the jungle, tearing through branches and vines, heedless of them grabbing at her, uncaring if any of them were snakes or not. *Mitch needed her.*

Gunshots continued to ring out from the front of the building. The remaining soldiers were plenty panicked. They must think the entire American army had invaded.

"The second Predator will be on target in four minutes, Kinsey. As soon as it gets there, we'll give them something more to think about."

As she approached the back of the building, the

gunshots out front subsided. Not good. The danger to this plan was that the bad guys would get a moment's pause and use it to blow away Mitch. She had to keep the pressure on these guys. She aimed at a small transformer box mounted high on a pole behind the building.

Darn it! She missed! She took another try at it. A shower of sparks erupted from the paint-can-size box. The lights inside the building flickered and went out. The air conditioner rumbled to a halt, and silence fell momentarily.

Then, to her vast relief, another fusillade of gunfire erupted from in front of the building. She fired as Hathaway had instructed her to at the roof of the metal building. The sound of her shots and the ping of metal would convince the bad guys that someone was firing back at them. In the chaos of their own shooting, they should have a hard time determining where the shots were coming from and what they were aimed at. Fortunately, the jungle was known to do weird things to sound.

Indeed, immediately after she squeezed off a couple rounds high—she surely didn't want to accidentally shoot Mitch through the flimsy walls of the building— a renewed frenzy of shooting erupted out front.

Her heart pounding so hard it hurt, she eased forward. Lord, she felt naked past the cover of the thick undergrowth. Who'd have thought she'd actually embrace the vines and brambles and threat of nasty critters the jungle represented? But here she was, wishing it went right up to the back of the building. She darted forward and crouched beside the air-conditioning unit and the low screen where its ducting entered the building.

Using the wire cutters she'd found in Mitch's bag of toys, she started snipping at the screen.

"Take a couple shots, Kinsey. They're getting bored out front."

She started. God bless the guys in the Bat Cave. She'd been so intent on getting to Mitch, she'd momentarily forgotten about distracting the Cubans at the front door. She fired a couple shots up at the roof.

As the rat-a-tat of gunfire duly started up again, she continued snipping. It was painfully slow work. Her hands ached dreadfully from the force of having to squeeze through the heavy wire, but she gritted her teeth and kept cutting. She remembered to pause to shoot again the next time, herself. She held the weapon clumsily and accidentally held the trigger down longer than she intended. A barrage of fire spewed from her weapon, all but knocking it from her hands. *Whoa.* She dropped it, startled.

Must keep moving. Must free Mitch. She picked up the wire cutters and went back to work. Almost there. A few more inches and she'd be able to bend the wire back and slip between the fan inside and the wall. It would be a tight squeeze, but Mitch was in there. She'd make it work.

"Target lock-in on the clearing in front of the building," Hathaway announced in her ear. "Cease fire, Kinsey. Let's see if we can draw a couple of these guys outside."

She kept snipping frantically.

"Bingo," Hathaway bit out in grim satisfaction. "Two tangoes have exited the building. Fire when ready."

Perfect. The idea was for the folks in the Bat Cave to release another missile and cause a big diversion so she could slip into the building and find Mitch.

She wrestled the screen up and away from the opening, cutting her palms on its sharp edges, completely oblivious to the searing pain. On her hands and knees, she waited for Hathaway's command.

Kaboom!

"Go, Kinsey."

She slipped through the opening, careful not to snag her clothes on the screen. Dust choked her, and spiderwebs coated her face. She couldn't get a hand up to wipe it away, but that was the least of her worries. For a brief, panicked moment, she got stuck between the ducting and the galvanized metal wall, but then the sheet metal flexed slightly and she was able to wriggle forward again. She had no idea how Mitch was going to get through this narrow gap. They'd cross that bridge when they got to it. The first order of business was to find him and free him.

The interior of the building was black. She couldn't see anything more than the barest of shapes. She pushed up to her hands and knees, hugging the wall. A brief flash of gunfire from outside faintly illuminated the doorway across the structure. It looked like a single open room. But in that brief moment, she didn't see Mitch. Had all of this been for nothing? Was he not here after all? Had she made a horrible mistake?

As her stomach sank, she heard a noise. An odd rasping sound. And a stab of agony so intense it stopped her breath shot through her lungs. *Mitch.*

She listened carefully. Another labored rasp. Off to her left. She darted that way, staying low. She kicked something hard and a grunt of pain sounded directly in front of her. She reached out in front of her with both hands. Cloth. The curve of a shoulder. A muscular one.

"Mitch?" she breathed. She thought his name as much as said it, so terrified was she that they were not alone in here.

No answer. Either he was unconscious, or he had a reason not to make any noise. Pain coursed through her freely. She instinctively knew he was experiencing the same pain, which meant he had to be conscious. She moved around behind him, crouching with his chair between her and the door. Easing the knife out of her waistband, she began sawing at the cords holding his wrists. It was hard to do in the dark. She couldn't see what she was doing and was terrified she would slit his wrists with the wickedly sharp blade. The bonds were tight and swollen with moisture.

But, grimly, she continued to saw. A cord popped. Then another. It felt like maybe there were two more strands wrapped around his wrists. But then his hands jerked and the bonds fell away.

The chair lurched gently. *His feet*. They must have bound his ankles to the chair.

She lay down, reaching forward under the chair to saw off the ropes around his legs. This was easier, for only the chair leg was behind the rope. Quickly, she released his right ankle, and then his left. She was startled when he didn't stand up.

He still wasn't talking, so he must think they weren't alone in here. Crud. As hard as she listened and as intently as she stared around into the darkness, she couldn't make out anyone else. She felt Mitch moving just a little, then realized he was picking at his chest. They must have tied his torso to the chair, too. She reached up behind him and made quick work of those ropes, as well.

And still he didn't move. Flummoxed, she crouched behind him, motionless. What was she supposed to do now? She'd assumed he'd take over from here, but he was just sitting there, not moving!

For lack of anything else to do, she eased the MP-4 upward very slowly, edging it forward along the side of the chair, up and under Mitch's right elbow. Its weight abruptly lifted out of her hands and she sagged with relief. Mitch continued to ease it forward by slow degrees. She marveled at his patience. She was on the verge of screaming in terror and frustration, her nerves stretched to the breaking point and beyond.

She started violently as a male voice mumbled in the dark...*in Spanish.*

A second voice answered.

Crap! They sounded like they were near the front door.

She heard a faint shuffle of shoes on concrete. Mitch's captors were moving. Where, she had no idea. She couldn't see a thing back here behind this chair. And now that she'd passed the MP-4 to Mitch, she was unarmed anyway, except for her knife. Fat lot of good that would do against these guys' guns.

A wave of helplessness washed over her. She hated this feeling! She was not giving in. They'd come this far, and they'd get out of here alive.

She jumped violently as Mitch fired his weapon without warning, a bright muzzle flash accompanying the deafening report of the weapon inside the building's metal walls.

Someone screamed, and the chair lurched violently to the side as Mitch flung himself off it. It occurred to her that she had better move, too, because the bad guys were bound to fire back at where Mitch's muzzle flash had just given away his position. She dived right, rolling fast for the nearest wall.

A hard hand closed over her mouth, and something heavy rolled on top of her. But then she recognized the muscular, familiar contours of Mitch's body against hers.

"Get out however you got in. Tell Hathaway these are Zaragosa's men. Zaragosa is in league with Camarillo and has turned on us. They've called for reinforcements. I'll hold them off as long as I can. Buy you time to run."

She froze in shock, absorbing all that in the blink of an eye.

A fusillade of gunfire lit up the front of the room.

"Move," Mitch grunted as he rolled off her and fired back. She scrambled toward the hole in the back wall, with Mitch close behind.

There was no cover in here. As soon as the Cubans just opened fire and sprayed the heck out of the space, she and Mitch were both dead. She paused before the narrow slit. Mitch would never fit through here. From somewhere behind her, Mitch fired his weapon. She felt as much as heard his dive and roll across the floor as pain exploded in her body.

"We need a diversion. *Now,*" she muttered into her microphone.

"Coming up. Fire the second missile."

She tugged frantically at the metal duct, trying to widen the space so Mitch could escape.

The ground rocked and a blast of light and heat rocked the building. Mitch skidded to the floor beside her. He reached up, pushed her hands aside and ripped the entire air-conditioning duct free of the wall, greatly enlarging the hole as debris banged down on the building's roof.

"Go," Mitch ordered.

"Not without you."

He gave her a push and she stubbornly shook her head.

"Fine. We both go." He sounded plenty mad, but like he also realized arguing with her would be futile. She paused, peering at him, trying to make out his expression.

"I swear," he bit out.

She dived through the now wide-open hole and rolled to her knees. A big burst of gunfire erupted inside, then Mitch's muscular body burst through the opening beside her. They took off running, diving to the ground in the first heavy tangle of jungle.

Grimly, Mitch took off crawling low on his belly. She followed, marveling that he could still move with such speed in the condition he—they—were in. She could really stop experiencing all his aches and pains any time, now.

He didn't go far, though, before he pulled up, leaning heavily against a tree trunk. She opened her mouth to ask him if he was okay, but he gestured her to silence and pointed at his ear. Ahh. He was listening for pursuit. She crouched stock-still, straining to hear any sound not of the jungle. She didn't know what the heck she was listening for, though.

He reached over and took the earbud and its attached mouthpiece out of her ear.

"I'm out. With Kinsey," he reported low.

He listened intently for a moment. "Roger."

Without speaking to her, he took off through the

jungle. At least they were able to walk upright this time. As grueling as the next half hour was, she couldn't complain. She'd had enough wallowing around in the mud with the bugs for one night.

Finally, Mitch stopped, sliding to the ground, panting himself. Her pain was nearly unbearable, and she was only experiencing ghost pains of his. She couldn't imagine the agony he was suffering.

"Take the headset, Kinsey. The folks in the cave will vector you out of here."

"What are you going to be doing?"

He started to laugh, but it turned into a gasp of pain. "I'm going to sit here and rest a while. Then I'm going to hook up with the SEAL team when it gets here. We've got an appointment with Camarillo and Zaragosa."

"I'm staying with you."

"Kinsey—"

"I'm not arguing with you about this. We're in this together."

He glared at her as balefully as he could from between the puffy slits of his eyes.

She squatted down in front of him and looked him square in the face. "You may think it's okay to walk away, Mitch, but I don't. Do you hear me? I'm *not* walking away. This time we're playing by *my* rules."

There, in the dark and the wet and fear, the jungle pressing in around them, their gazes met. Very slowly, his cracked and blackened lips curved up. She felt the pain of the smile in her own mouth. He leaned forward. Reached up with his right hand to grab a fistful of her shirt. He dragged her forward until their noses almost touched.

"Yeah. I hear you. Your rules from now on."

She stared. "Do you mean it?"

His other hand came up behind her head, pulling her the last few inches separating them and their two worlds. "I promise."

"Your word of honor?"

"My word of honor. I'm never walking away from you again."

On a sob, she gathered him in her arms, careful of his injuries. His arms wrapped painfully tight around her, but she didn't complain. She slid down to the ground beside him, still holding him. As she felt his consciousness slipping away, she said gently, "Give me the radio." She added, "And the gun."

With his last strength, he dragged the earpiece off his head and passed her the weapon.

"I'll take the watch," she murmured. "You rest now. I've got your back."

"I love the sound of that. I love you," he sighed. And then he passed out.

She stared down at his dark head. He loved her! Exultation exploded within her. She wanted to kiss him madly, to make passionate love with him, to sing and shout her joy, and the man had just passed out cold.

There'd be time enough later to share their love. A lifetime. Smiling, she donned the headset and laid the gun at the ready across her lap.

And all was right with the world. She sat there in the mud and filth, with rain streaming down her face, aching in every last muscle, and so exhausted she could hardly see straight. Mitch's head was heavy on her shoulder, his battered body draped uncomfortably over hers. And none of it mattered. The spy, the trained predator and the pampered princess had found each other. They'd become a team. A heck of a good one if she did say so herself. And neither of them would ever have to be alone again.

And as she sat there, the first birds of dawn began to sing and the sun rose on a new day. They'd found their way out of the darkness. Together.

Chapter 14

Not quite one week later, Mitch shifted uncomfortably in his chair, the bandage binding his broken ribs itching across his back. Kinsey reached up absently from the seat beside him and used her newly manicured nails to scratch the spot below his shoulder blades. How she did that, he couldn't begin to fathom, but she seemed to know exactly how he felt, to be aware of every ache or pain before he was barely aware of it himself.

After she'd eased the itch, he captured her fingers and carried them up to his mouth to kiss them briefly. She glanced away from the satellite imagery on the big screen in front of them and flashed him a smile of pure love.

Her beauty, both inside and out, made his breath catch in the back of his throat. What he'd ever done to deserve a woman like her he couldn't imagine, but he wasn't about to question his good luck. Hell, his great luck. He was the luckiest man alive. Not only had he cheated death in a major way in Cuba, but he'd fallen for Kinsey Hollingsworth, and miraculously, she'd fallen for him.

"What are they doing now?" she asked.

He glanced up at the screen where the SEAL team was preparing to launch a very quiet, very lethal assault on Camarillo's compound. Zaragosa had been confirmed entering the main house ten minutes earlier, and the SEALs, who'd been in place for the past several days, were closing in for the kill. "They're separating so they won't shoot each other if it comes to a firefight."

Kinsey grinned. "You can tell me they're managing their fields of fire. I know what that means now."

His eyebrows lifted. "Are you sure you want to become a field operative? When I talked to your father last night, he said he'd unfrozen all your bank accounts and has signed your entire trust fund over to you. You're a wealthy lady now."

"I'm sure. Good thing you proposed to me yesterday morning. I know you're not marrying me for my money."

He leaned over close and whispered, "If you came to me with nothing in the world but your name, I'd still want you. I don't know what your ex-fiancé was thinking, cheating on you. Damn goof. You sure you don't want me to kill him?"

She smiled gently. "Thanks for the offer, but no. If he needs killing, I'll do it myself. And speaking of exes, do you need me to take out Janine?"

He shrugged. "Na. I owe her one. If she hadn't dumped me, I'd never have found you."

She reached behind his neck and drew him close

enough to kiss. "God bless Janine for not knowing what she had."

He all but purred under her hand.

"What about Hunter?" she asked.

Mitch shrugged. "He'll be eighteen next year. He says he wants to join the Army. I offered to help him out with college, but he seems to need more action than that."

Kinsey laughed. "Are you sure he's not yours?"

A shadow passed over Mitch's happiness. At least he was talking about his past now. Between the two of them they'd get beyond the ghosts lurking in his history. She reached out with her fingertips to smooth his eyebrow. "I love you," she murmured.

He gazed back at her solemnly. "I love you, too."

A throat cleared significantly nearby. Abruptly, Mitch recalled where they were and that they'd had an audience. A large one.

Kinsey blushed, and he caught Jennifer Blackfoot's knowing smile from across the table. He grinned back at her. She'd been hassling him for years to find a good woman and settle down. Looked like the boss got her wish. As Jennifer opened her mouth, a mischievous glint in her eye, he cut off the poke he saw coming and said, "So when are you going to take the plunge?"

Jennifer drew back sharply. "Not me. I'm not the type. Wrong job. Wrong lifestyle. No time."

He nodded knowingly. "That's what I said. And look what happened to me."

He looped an arm around Kinsey's shoulder and reveled at how she snuggled close to his side.

"There he goes," Hathaway commented, drawing Mitch's gaze back to the screen. One of the SEALs had broken away from the main group and was making his way with surprising speed toward the heating and cooling units behind the main house.

Camarillo's compound was about to suffer a most unfortunate natural gas explosion that would vaporize all the occupants of the house. The last explosives were rigged, and then a quick double click came across the Bat Cave's loudspeaker system, which was broadcasting the SEALs' operational frequency at the moment.

The team withdrew as silently as it had come, retreating a safe distance back into the jungle.

Hathaway looked over at Kinsey from his place at the ops console. "Would you like to do the honors?" he asked.

She smiled over at Mitch, then leaned forward and pushed the button on the speakerphone on the table in front of her. "Fire at will, gentlemen."

An enormous explosion filled the screen, momentarily whiting out the satellite feed. Then a giant blaze came into focus. Smaller secondary explosions lit the night, and it became patently clear the SEALs had succeeded in their mission. No one was walking out of that conflagration alive.

"It's over," Kinsey breathed.

Mitch leaned over, drawing her close. "Oh, no. It's just begun. Now we can get on with our life—together."

And they kissed to seal the deal.

* * * * *

*Look for Cindy Dees's next romance
in August 2008
from Silhouette Romantic Suspense!*

Look for LAST WOLF WATCHING
by Rhyannon Byrd—the exciting conclusion in the
BLOODRUNNERS miniseries
from Silhouette Nocturne.

Follow Michaela and Brody on their fierce journey to
find the truth and face the demons from the past,
as they reach the heart of the battle between
the Runners and the rogues.

Here is a sneak preview of book three,
LAST WOLF WATCHING.

Michaela squinted, struggling to see through the impenetrable darkness. Everyone looked toward the Elders, but she knew Brody Carter still watched her. Michaela could feel the power of his gaze. Its heat. Its strength. And something that felt strangely like anger, though he had no reason to have any emotion toward her. Strangers from different worlds, brought together beneath the heavy silver moon on a night made for hell itself. That was their only connection.

The second she finished that thought, she knew it was a lie. But she couldn't deal with it now. Not tonight. Not when her whole world balanced on the edge of destruction.

Willing her backbone to keep her upright, Michaela Doucet focused on the towering blaze of a roaring bonfire that rose from the far side of the clearing, its orange flames burning with maniacal zeal against the inky black curtain of the night. Many of the Lycans had already shifted into their preternatural shapes, their fur-covered bodies standing like monstrous shadows at the edges of the forest as they waited with restless expectancy for her brother.

Her nineteen-year-old brother, Max, had been attacked by a rogue werewolf—a Lycan who preyed upon humans for food. Max had been bitten in the attack, which meant he was no longer human, but a breed of creature that existed between the two worlds of man and beast, much like the Bloodrunners themselves.

The Elders parted, and two hulking shapes emerged from the trees. In their wolf forms, the Lycans stood over seven feet tall, their legs bent at an odd angle as they stalked forward. They each held a thick chain that had been wound around their inside wrists, the twin lengths leading back into the shadows. The Lycans had taken no more than a few steps when they jerked on the chains, and her brother appeared.

Bound like an animal.

Biting at her trembling lower lip, she glanced left, then right, surprised to see that others had joined her. Now the Bloodrunners and their family and friends stood as a united force against the Silvercrest pack, which had yet to accept the fact that something sinister was eating away at its foundation—something that would rip down the protective walls that separated their world from the humans'. It occurred to Michaela that loyalties were being announced tonight—a separation made between those who would stand with the Runners in their fight against the rogues and those who blindly supported the pack's refusal to face reality. But all she could focus on was her brother. Max looked so hurt...so terrified.

"Leave him alone," she screamed, her soft-soled, black satin slip-ons struggling for purchase in the damp earth as she rushed toward Max, only to find herself lifted off the ground when a hard, heavily muscled arm clamped around her waist from behind, pulling her clear off her feet. "Damn it, let me down!" she snarled, unable to take her eyes off her brother as the golden-eyed Lycan kicked him.

Mindless with heartache and rage, Michaela clawed at the arm holding her, kicking her heels against whatever part of her captor's legs she could reach. "Stop it," a deep, husky voice grunted in her ear. "You're not helping him by losing it. I give you my word he'll survive the ceremony, but you have to keep it together."

"Nooooo!" she screamed, too hysterical to listen to reason. "You're monsters! All of you! Look what you've done to him! How dare you! *How dare you!*"

The arm tightened with a powerful flex of muscle, cinching her waist. Her breath sucked in on a sharp, wailing gasp.

"Shut up before you get both yourself and your brother killed. I will *not* let that happen. Do you understand me?" her captor growled, shaking her so hard that her teeth clicked together. "Do you understand me, Doucet?"

"Damn it," she cried, stricken as she watched one of the guards grab Max by his hair. Around them Lycans huffed and growled as they watched the spectacle, while others outright howled for the show to begin.

"That's enough!" the voice seethed in her ear.

"They'll tear you apart before you even reach him, and I'll be damned if I'm going to stand here and watch you die."

Suddenly, through the haze of fear and agony and outrage in her mind, she finally recognized who'd caught her. *Brody.*

He held her in his arms, her body locked against his powerful form, her back to the burning heat of his chest. A low, keening sound of anguish tore through her, and her head dropped forward as hoarse sobs of pain ripped from her throat. "Let me go. I have to help him. *Please*," she begged brokenly, knowing only that she needed to get to Max. "Let me go, Brody."

He muttered something against her hair, his breath warm against her scalp, and Michaela could have sworn it was a single word…. But she must have heard wrong. She was too upset. Too furious. Too terrified. She must be out of her mind.

Because it sounded as if he'd quietly snarled the word *never.*

nocturne™

THE FINAL INSTALLMENT OF
THE BLOODRUNNERS TRILOGY

Last Wolf Watching

Runner Brody Carter has found his match in
Michaela Doucet, a human with unusual psychic powers.
When Michaela's brother is threatened, Brody becomes
her protector, and suddenly not only has to protect her
from her enemies but also from himself....

LOOK FOR

LAST WOLF WATCHING
BY

RHYANNON
BYRD

Available May 2008 wherever you buy books.

Dramatic and Sensual Tales of Paranormal Romance

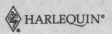
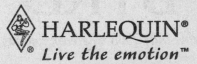

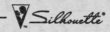

SPECIAL EDITION™

 THE WILDER FAMILY
Healing Hearts in Walnut River

Social worker Isobel Suarez was proud to
work at Walnut River General Hospital, so
when Neil Kane showed up from the attorney
general's office to investigate insurance fraud,
she was up in arms. Until she melted in his
arms, and things got very tricky...

Look for

HER MR. RIGHT?
by
KAREN ROSE SMITH

Available May wherever books are sold.

REQUEST YOUR FREE BOOKS!

2 FREE NOVELS PLUS 2 FREE GIFTS!

Silhouette® Romantic

SUSPENSE

Sparked by Danger, Fueled by Passion!

YES! Please send me 2 FREE Silhouette® Romantic Suspense novels and my 2 FREE gifts (gifts are worth about $10). After receiving them, if I don't wish to receive any more books, I can return the shipping statement marked "cancel." If I don't cancel, I will receive 4 brand-new novels every month and be billed just $4.24 per book in the U.S. or $4.99 per book in Canada, plus 25¢ shipping and handling per book plus applicable taxes, if any*. That's a savings of at least 15% off the cover price! I understand that accepting the 2 free books and gifts places me under no obligation to buy anything. I can always return a shipment and cancel at any time. Even if I never buy another book from Silhouette, the two free books and gifts are mine to keep forever.

240 SDN EEX6 340 SDN EEYJ

Name	(PLEASE PRINT)
Address	Apt. #
City	State/Prov. Zip/Postal Code

Signature (if under 18, a parent or guardian must sign)

Mail to the Silhouette Reader Service:
IN U.S.A.: P.O. Box 1867, Buffalo, NY 14240-1867
IN CANADA: P.O. Box 609, Fort Erie, Ontario L2A 5X3

Not valid to current subscribers of Silhouette Romantic Suspense books.

Want to try two free books from another line?
Call 1-800-873-8635 or visit www.morefreebooks.com.

* Terms and prices subject to change without notice. N.Y. residents add applicable sales tax. Canadian residents will be charged applicable provincial taxes and GST. This offer is limited to one order per household. All orders subject to approval. Credit or debit balances in a customer's account(s) may be offset by any other outstanding balance owed by or to the customer. Please allow 4 to 6 weeks for delivery. Offer available while quantities last.

Your Privacy: Silhouette is committed to protecting your privacy. Our Privacy Policy is available online at www.eHarlequin.com or upon request from the Reader Service. From time to time we make our lists of customers available to reputable third parties who may have a product or service of interest to you. If you would prefer we not share your name and address, please check here. ☐

SRS08

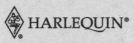

HARLEQUIN®

American ★ Romance®

Three Boys and a Baby

When Ella Garvey's eight-year-old twins and
their best friend, Dillon, discover an abandoned
baby girl, they fear she will be put in jail—
or worse! They decide to take matters into their
own hands and run away. Luckily the outlaws are
found quickly…and Ella finds a second chance
at love—with Dillon's dad, Jackson.

LOOK FOR

Three Boys and a Baby

BY

LAURA MARIE ALTOM

*Available May
wherever you buy books.*

LOVE, HOME & HAPPINESS

HARLEQUIN Presents

Look out for brilliant author

Susan Napier

in May 2008—
only in Harlequin Presents!

ACCIDENTAL
MISTRESS

#2729

One night Emily Quest is rescued by a handsome
stranger. Despite the heart–stopping attraction
between them, Emily thought she'd never see
him again. But now, years later, he is right in front
of her, as sexy as ever....

Don't miss Susan's next book in Harlequin
Presents—coming soon!

Silhouette®
Romantic
SUSPENSE

COMING NEXT MONTH

#1511 SECRET AGENT AFFAIR—Marie Ferrarella
The Doctors Pulaski
CIA agent Kane Donnelly thinks posing as an orderly to
monitor rumors of terrorist activity will be easy. Then he runs into
Dr. Marja Pulaski, the woman who saved his life only days prior. As
the investigation progresses he finds himself entangled with the feisty
resident, risking his heart—and possibly his mission.

#1512 THE GUARDIAN—Linda Winstead Jones
Last Chance Heroes
When Dante Mangino goes to investigate a panty theft, he doesn't expect
to wind up protecting his old flame, Mayor Sara Vance, from a stalker.
Dante refuses to get involved again. But as the danger to Sara escalates,
so does their simmering attraction. Now he must come to terms with old
feelings—and the one woman who captured his soul.

#1513 THE BLACK SHEEP P.I.—Karen Whiddon
The Cordasic Legacy
Accused of her husband's murder, Rachel Adair knows she must turn to
the one man who can help her...the same man she betrayed years ago.
Dominic Cordasic is stunned when his ex-fiancée walks through his door
seeking his help. He promised himself he'd cut this woman from his life
completely, yet he can't say no to her plea. Worse yet, he may still love
her.

#1514 HEART OF A THIEF—Gail Barrett
The Crusaders
When the legendary necklace security expert Luke Moreno agreed to
safeguard goes missing, he has a hunch it has something to do with his
former lover, amber expert Sofia Mikhelson. Framed for a crime she
didn't commit, Sofia doesn't know who she can trust, but must team up
with Luke if she wants to survive. But how can she stay so close to the
only man she's ever loved, the same man who believes she's set him
up—again?